A Guidebook to Monsters

A Guidebook to Monsters

Philosophy, Religion, and the Paranormal

Ryan J. Stark

CASCADE *Books* • Eugene, Oregon

A GUIDEBOOK TO MONSTERS
Philosophy, Religion, and the Paranormal

Cascade Books
An Imprint of Wipf and Stock Publishers
199 W. 8th Ave., Suite 3
Eugene, OR 97401

www.wipfandstock.com

PAPERBACK ISBN: 978-1-6667-8469-5
HARDCOVER ISBN: 978-1-6667-8470-1
EBOOK ISBN: 978-1-6667-8471-8

Cataloguing-in-Publication data:

Names: Stark, Ryan J. [author].

Title: A guidebook to monsters : philosophy, religion, and the paranormal / by Ryan J. Stark.

Description: Eugene, OR: Cascade Books, 2024 | Includes bibliographical references and index.

Identifiers: ISBN 978-1-6667-8469-5 (paperback) | ISBN 978-1-6667-8470-1 (hardcover) | ISBN 978-1-6667-8471-8 (ebook)

Subjects: LCSH: Monsters | Monsters in mass media | Monsters in literature | Monsters in motion pictures | Monsters—Fiction | Monsters in popular culture | Religion and culture | Philosophy

Classification: PS374.M544 S73 2024 (paperback) | PS374.M544 (ebook)

VERSION NUMBER 02/19/24

Contents

Acknowledgments

God bless Ashley Kunsa, Cathy Kemp, Tina Skouen, Bill Feuer, Joe Pappa, Kent Kersey, Evan Hedlund, Colette Tennant, Felicia Squires, Allen Jones, Naomi Yanike, Laurie Smith, Ceri McLardy, Rebecca Clintworth, and DeAnna Thomas. I also thank my family for their encouragement, my fantastic students for their camaraderie, and Wipf and Stock's dedicated staff for their knowhow and good humor: George Callihan, Matt Wimer, Robin Parry (editor), Karl Coppock (proofreader), Rachel Saunders (typesetter), and Shannon Carter (cover designer).

Introduction

JOHN DURANT, LIGHT OF the British Science Association, put *The X-Files* on his public dangers list.[1] The reason: it glamorized the supernatural. Many of his colleagues shared the sentiment, unnerved as they were by Agent Scully's return to her lapsed Catholicism upon encountering the paranormal. And they were right to be unnerved. Encounters with the paranormal change people, in fiction and in fact. Or, in other words, those who watch *The X-Files* do put themselves in peril, much like those who read these chapters. Not that skeptics should retreat, of course, but this book comes with a playful warning nonetheless, one that C. S. Lewis issued to himself as a young atheist. After finding the Romantics, after discerning for the first time the world's high strangeness, he observed, "A young man who wishes to remain a sound atheist cannot be too careful of his reading."[2]

If not *The X-Files*, then *Twin Peaks* and *Buffy the Vampire Slayer*. Or ghostly *Hamlet*, preternatural *Moby Dick*, and all those shelves of tattered dime-store comic books. And the late-night creature features, too, which carry a realism that the modern realists have long-since forgotten. Realism is not what it used to be. In the old days, before the internet, before the printing press, the hard-bitten villagers understood first principles, one of which goes as follows: the monsters are real. They always have been, and to

1. Aldersey-Williams, *In Search of Thomas Browne*, 166.

2. Lewis, *Surprised by Joy*, 185.

know as much is to know more than those who would close their eyes and wish away the horror.

Of the kinds of monsters at large, I have—for our purposes—identified eight, each of which appears in a separate chapter with a self-explanatory title. "Vampires," "Leviathans," et cetera. Collected together, these chapters provide a counter-narrative to conventional academic wisdom on the topic, which, as a general rule, presupposes the monsters to be metaphors, full of symbolic import but nothing beyond that.[3] More recently, some scholars—in an effort to transcend the purely figurative—describe monsterdom as "phenomenologically actual," which means that those who see the creatures perceive them to be real.[4] And with good reason, presumably, unless they hallucinate or, worse yet, fall prey to a hoax. Still, the term "actual" by itself produces the best effect, I think, as in "the monsters are actual" per the hard-bitten villagers and their old-fashioned realism, but such a phrasing brings with it supernatural and paranormal frameworks that inevitably invite intrigue. Here, then, is why the subject lends itself so provocatively to philosophical conversation. The question of monsters is a question of metaphysics.

Not that we should expect readers to believe in monsters, nor should we anticipate forthcoming proofs in manuscripts. The monsters themselves either will or will not confirm their presence. In the meanwhile, this book constitutes a series of efforts to characterize the entities properly and, in another register, to deliver a measure of comic relief, which might seem out of place in a discourse about often-demonic events. But—to invoke Thomas More and Martin Luther—the instruments of darkness hate mirth.[5] If we should happen to undercut Hell's incessant gravity, then all the better. If this work proves too irreverent, however, then something has gone wrong. The intent, here, is otherwise. If it proves too short, then I recall Mark Twain's memorable adage that no sinner

3. Beal, *Religion and Its Monsters*; Cowan, *Magic, Monsters, and Make-Believe Heroes*; Braudy, *Haunted*; Asma, *On Monsters*.

4. Laycock and Mikles, "Monster Theory and Religious Studies," 3–16.

5. Cited in Lewis, *The Screwtape Letters*, viii.

was ever saved after the first twenty minutes of a sermon. And if these chapters seem too weird, then all I can say is that I have read the Bible, and they are not as weird as that curious book.

1

Vampires

Peace, n.: a period of scheming between two periods of violence.

—*The Devil's Dictionary*

LITERARY HISTORIANS POINT TO John Polidori's *The Vampyre* (1819) as that key moment in Western vampire lore when the grisly undead creature found himself transformed into something more sophisticated. Lord Ruthven, the suave vampire in question, seduces young women and orchestrates chaos in the lives of others, all for his own carnal pleasure. Importantly, he does this by way of persuasion, not rote coercion, which illustrates a key aspect of the modern vampire's modus operandi. He prefers romance to compulsion, seduction to force. He prefers thrall, almost to the end, at which point the monster fully emerges and the victims fully grasp that their good senses have been compromised, but by then it is too late.

"None are more hopelessly enslaved than those who falsely believe they are free," Goethe once observed.[1] Similarly, none are

1. Goethe, *Opinions*, 3.

more hopelessly enslaved than those who believe themselves to be dating vampires.

Exactly what constitutes thrall is a murky affair insofar as thrall is a lot like hypnosis, if not the same thing, and of this phenomenon we know very little. Agent Scully and Jose Chung make the point in a memorable exchange on the topic from *The X-Files*, season 2:

> Chung: The C.I.A., when conducting their MK-Ultra mind control experiments back in the 50s, had no idea how hypnosis worked. Or what it was.
>
> Scully: No one still knows.
>
> Chung: Still, as a storyteller, I'm fascinated by how a person's sense of consciousness can be so transformed by nothing more magical than listening to words. Mere words.[2]

And many have fallen prey to such words. Buffy the vampire slayer succumbs to thrall, for example, so much so that she invites Dracula to bite her, and he happily obliges, if "happily" is possible in the mind of a vampire.[3] Later, having sobered up from the ordeal, Buffy stakes the villain, but we are nonetheless left with an uneasy feeling. Despite all her experience, despite all her kung-fu know-how, Buffy still crumbles in the wake of thrall, at least temporarily, putting herself in grave danger and eliciting from us a pressing set of questions. How could this have happened so easily? Will this happen again? Are women attracted to men in capes?

Much like kryptonite, vampire magic also affects Superman. Two vampires have so far succeeded in hypnotizing him. Crucifer, not fortunate in name, enthralls our protagonist and sends him on several errands, until the Man of Steel has a moment of clarity, as the alcoholics call it, at which point he punches the ancient vampire through the heart while holding a wooden cross in his fist, just to make doubly sure.[4] Dracula, too, disguised as an aris-

2. Carter, "Jose Chung's *From Outer Space*," season 3, episode 20.
3. Whedon, "Buffy vs Dracula," season 5, episode 1.
4. Byrne and Claremont, "Enemy Within," volume 1, issue 95.

tocrat named Rominoff, charms our superhero rather easily and then bites him on the neck, only to explode—hilariously—on the premise that Superman's blood is tinged with sunlight, a moment of dream logic used to subvert the expectation that superblood might somehow benefit the Count.[5]

Lord Ruthven of Polidori fame also wanders into the DC Comic Book Universe and, per usual, charms his way through problems, until he inadvertently skewers himself on a war memorial.[6] Before this happens, however, we get the strong impression that Ruthven could beguile Superman with ease, if given the chance: that pens are mightier than swords and always have been.

Now is a good time to mention, too, that the critics are wrong about Polidori and the modern vampire mythos. An earlier episode precedes Ruthven by nearly fifty years and involves the priest and novelist Laurence Sterne, to whom the Romantics looked for inspiration, Polidori among them. The scenario is as follows: in 1770, the publisher Richard Griffith printed some gossip about Sterne and a younger married woman named Eliza Draper, for whom the famous writer pined in his semi-autobiographical *Journal to Eliza*. Also married, much older, and dying of tuberculosis, Sterne took an unhealthy interest in Draper, and she, him, which caused Griffith—through a literary pseudonym—to wonder aloud if the two had fallen in love, even if momentarily. But Griffith then quickly dismisses the indecorous speculation:

> In truth, there was nothing in the affair worth making a secret of—the world that knew of their correspondence knew the worst of it, which was merely a simple folly. Any other idea of the matter would be more than the most abandoned vice could render probable. To intrigue with a vampire! To sink into the arms of death alive![7]

Of course, vampires were not the dreamy seducers they turned out to be after Polidori and especially Bram Stoker; on the contrary,

5. Loeb and Johns, "House of Dracula," volume 2, issue 180.
6. Jurgens, "Raising the Stakes," volume 2, issue 70.
7. Griffith, *Genuine Letters*, 200.

they were inarticulate monsters, inconsistent with Sterne's graceful persona—often described as the quintessential "man of feeling."[8] And, straightforwardly, Griffith leaves it there, with Sterne's sentimentality intact. But in another register, we discover—here—an oddly prescient moment of misdirection, or what the rhetoricians call a paralipsis: Griffith provides for readers a nightmare vision of the sensitive but now-corrupted religious man turned vampire, who then preys upon a naïve young woman, the unsuspecting victim, Eliza. He seems to pass over the vision in silence, as if not to contemplate it, but the exclamation mark proves otherwise. "To sink into the arms of death alive!" Such is the quintessential vampire gestalt, before Lord Ruthven and Count Dracula. Such is an unexpected precursor to the modern vampire mythos.

Psychoanalysts observe that to empathize with sociopaths is to negate the self most dangerously. They are right, I think, and right, too, that self-erasure proves difficult to recognize at times—because it feels like love. As if we are to save the vampires. As if we can. But observant philosophers have warned against such misplaced empathy from the start. As the early church fathers tell us, those who dine with the devils should bring long spoons.[9] In other words, we are to behave with skepticism toward evil, and herein lies the deeper pathology behind courtships with vampires. Such intimacies do not convert them, but instead put us in peril—like the "woman wailing for her demon-lover" in Coleridge's "Kubla Kahn."[10] She has a death wish, Freud might say, but it seems more like a savior syndrome in the final analysis.[11] Like so many who commune with the devils, she hopes to redeem the irredeemable, but only Christ can enter the gates of Hell unaffected, undeterred, and so preach to the dead—as the author of 1 Peter 4:6 describes. We cannot. We might rightly and reasonably hope for the restoration of all things, but if we throw our arms around the demonic,

8. Greene, "'Man of Feeling' Reconsidered," 159–83.

9. Lewis, "Inner Ring," 56.

10. Coleridge, *Poetical Works*, 143–46.

11. Freud, *Beyond the Pleasure Principle*, 53.

then we misunderstand evil's ontology and our relationship to it. The vampires are not ours to save.

When Peter rebuked Christ in Matthew 16, having not comprehended the prophecy of Christ's death and resurrection, Jesus turned to him and said, "Get behind me, Satan!" We find a clue, here, for how we might respond to vampires who would have us participate in their own dissent. Relatedly, reports have it that Luther once threw an inkwell at an evil spirit in his study; it was an effort to chase off the grim creature, apparently. If the well hit the demon we do not know, but that Luther tried is what matters.[12]

Vampires play their part in reality's anti-masque, that shadow narrative of spiritual warfare running alongside God's unstoppable plan to rescue the world. They perform dreadful rites and promise to their acolytes an immortality that is not theirs to give, an immortality that already exists. The vampire's affectation extends also to their eloquence, which is backwardly liturgical. The bow of pretended humility, the elongated gesture, the brooding gravity—all produce together a bizarre carriage of the body that conceals a sinister carriage of the mind. Even in hospitality the vampire exaggerates, like the Macbeths as they welcome King Duncan to the Castle: "All our service," the lady says, "in every point twice done and then done double."[13] As a case in point, recall the embroidered hospitality of Bela Lugosi's 1931 Dracula, caught between silent film and sound: "I bid you welcome," he says, acting out the part as if the audience must see his intentions through dramatic gestures.[14] A perfect moment when the silent cinema and talking pictures conspire to produce the quintessential vampire ethos, an overstated affectation captured for the modern age.

And if photographs of real vampires were possible, as opposed to photographs of movie star vampires, then we would find exactly none in which the creature smiles naturally, because they cannot do so, no matter how forcefully they will it. In this way, vampires are akin to the possessed Prince Rilian in C. S. Lewis's

12. Hendrix, *Martin Luther*, 4.

13. Shakespeare, *Macbeth*, 1.6.18–19.

14. Browning, *Dracula*.

The Silver Chair, who—when attempting to laugh—carries only a contorted expression on his face, as Jill rightly notices. She cannot pinpoint the problem, but knows enough to know that she must not trust a man incapable of real laughter.[15]

The vampire's body, too, is equally manufactured by some dark magic, which becomes readily apparent at the moment of demise, where a stake through the heart, or a beam of sunlight through a window pane, profoundly ages the monster, leaving in its wake a handful of dust. With the spell broken, the vampire's phantasmagorical body disappears into the ether, a final proof of its occult origin, if the problem of non-reflection in all the world's mirrors was not proof enough.

Some speculate that if vampires were able to see themselves in mirrors, they would reconsider their wardrobes. We have reason to think otherwise. Of course, the true gothic is not the vampire aesthetic, because the true gothic always points to Heaven, as in Notre Dame Cathedral, for instance, or Westminster Abbey. On the contrary, vampires have a long history of not pointing to Heaven. Instead, they gild the lily. In their attempt to out-gothic the gothic, they turn their style inwardly upon themselves, *incurvatus in se*, which signals not grandeur but rather self-apotheosis. In essence, vampires are their own cathedrals, and with this premise proceed accordingly, candelabras in tow.

Longinus, in *On the Sublime*, rightly uses the term "frigidity" to describe the emotional effect produced by such false grandeur—aka failed sublimity.[16] He means to convey both rhetorical and metaphysical coldness, as does Dante, who has the Devil frozen in a block of ice at the Inferno's frigid and gaudy center. As does Stanley Kubrick, too, who freezes the possessed Jack in the maze at the end of *The Shining*. And somewhere nearby the frozen middle of Hell we find the rooms of vampires, those who betrayed the strangers in their midst and preyed upon the lonely and the desperate. Their "fangs are knives," per Proverbs 30:14, used "to devour the poor from off the earth," but now they devour only

15. Lewis, *Silver Chair*, 124.

16. Longinus, *On the Sublime*, 25.

themselves. As the wise theologians often say, we are punished by our sins, not for them.

On a side note, and concerning the vampire's many choristers, the opening scene of Lugosi's 1931 *Dracula* features three armadillos. They wander about the castle and mind their own business, it seems, as wolves howl and spiders weave their webs. From where did they come? How did they get there? Are they angels in disguise? Regardless, the armadillos further confirm Longinus's additional point that the ridiculous and the sublime bear a family resemblance.

What, then, are we to make of the vampires who sparkle and the vampires with souls? Or, if not in the direction of the dreamy, then in the theater of the absurd: Count Chocula, the mascot for a popular breakfast cereal, or the puppet Count von Count from the children's program *Sesame Street*, who teaches viewers how to add and subtract—hitting all the numbers with his heavy Transylvanian accent. We might deem these manifestations too unserious to be taken seriously, but in fairness to the spirit of Count Chocula, perhaps something else happens here. Namely, we find more variations upon the culture-making effort to rehabilitate the demonic, and the almost demonic, as the case might be. If the vampire could only find pleasure in chocolate, if he could laugh with children, if he could be loved like Bella loves Edward in *The Twilight Saga*, then maybe there is hope enough in the world for all of us. Indeed, maybe some vampires have grown tired of being vampires. That said, we also do well to heed the old Transylvanian proverb, lest we over-empathize with the villains: the sane would do no good if they made themselves vampires to help the vampires.

A recent meme depicts the real Dracula in the company of Count Chocula, Count von Count, *The Twilight Saga*'s Edward, and several other less-than-scary princes of darkness, at which point Dracula laments that the vampires have lost their edge.

And, true, I have yet to comment on psychic vampires and flaming extroverts, which is an oversight to be sure. As a corrective, and by way of conclusion, I observe the following: for twenty-seven dollars, one can buy a beaker of psychic vampire repellent from Gwyneth Paltrow's Goop Store in Beverly Hills, California.

The Paper Crane Apothecary makes the product, which—with an essential blend of rosemary, lavender, and juniper—protects against the fiends who corner people at parties. At present, however, shipping will be difficult: the website tells me "This item is sold out."

2

Werewolves

Where there is a monster there is a miracle.

—*Ogden Nash*

THE FIRST METAMORPHOSIS IN Ovid's *Metamorphosis* is an unhappy one. We see Jupiter transform King Lycaon into a wolf, a scene to which those who study werewolves often point as an early example of the man-beast's pedigree. Of course, Jupiter has good reason: Lycaon dabbles in cannibalism and child sacrifice, which sets in motion the bad king's emblematic punishment. John Dryden translates the key passage as such:

> [Lycaon's] mantle, now his hide, with rugged hairs
> Cleaves to his back; a famished face he bears;
> His arms descend, his shoulders sink away
> To multiply his legs for chase of prey.
> He grows a wolf, his hoariness remains,
> And the same rage in other members reigns.
> His eyes still sparkle in a narrower space:
> His jaws retain the grin, and violence of his face.[1]

1. Dryden, *Miscellaneous Works*, 338–39.

Not coincidentally, what follows Ovid's account is the story of the Great Deluge, that cataclysm by water firmly implanted in humankind's collective memory, from the Inuit to the Pima, from Dan to Beersheba. The earth was corrupt and full of violence, the author of Genesis 6 tells us, and then came the werewolves.[2] And then the Flood.

The Anunnaki kings were said to have reigned for thirty thousand years per king, give or take, by the count of those mysterious Sumerian tablets on display in the British Museum. Methuselah lived nine hundred years, while Noah was six hundred when the Flood descended. By contrast, the life expectancy of *canis dirus*, the fearsome dog, is around twelve years. And in those twelve years we may discover a portent about time and the human condition. Namely, there is as much danger for regress as for progress in history, a theme developed at that key point in *The Magician's Nephew* where Aslan instructs the talking animals to behave respectfully toward the beasts of the field: "Treat them gently and cherish them but do not go back to their ways lest you cease to be Talking Beasts."[3] His point is very much like that of Thomas Hobbes's: in the absence of a good society, we are told in *Leviathan*, life becomes "poor, nasty, brutish, and short."[4]

As a definitional matter, what constitutes a werewolf seems not terribly complicated, at least not usually. They are a particular sect of the occasionally transmogrified, like the Dr. Jekylls and Mr. Hydes of the world, or the Bruce Banners and Incredible Hulks. In contrast, we disqualify the Beast from the X-Men franchise, mainly on the grounds that his beast form and his natural form are one and the same. So too with Spiderman, the Cynocephali, Anubis, the Egyptian god of mummification, and Squirrel Girl, who marshals the power of the squirrel. The Beast from *Beauty and the Beast* presents a variation upon the theme, however, insofar as he maintains a permanent beastly shape throughout the story, until love finally lifts the curse in the end, at which point he returns to

2. Genesis 6:11.

3. Lewis, *Magician's Nephew*, 124.

4. Hobbes, *Leviathan*, 62.

human form. But even as a beast, the prince seems not to have lost his mind, only his body, which consists of a wolf's legs and tail, a buffalo's head, a bear's torso, a lion's mane, and two tusks from a boar. Indeed, he is a pastiche of a creature, not a werewolf proper, and not a werewolf at all in mind, or mental capacity.

Nor should we count the world's shape-shifters as werewolves, those trickster dogs of ancient Chinese lore, for example, and the Transylvanian vampires who become wolves at will, or bats, or colonies of rats. They transmogrify strategically, not cursedly, and so do not suffer the man-wolf's specific unholy condition. And neither do those who seek out profane transformation, the killers who would be dragons, for instance, and the mayors who would be demon serpents, as in the case of Sunnydale's Richard Wilkins III, who maintains his small-town politeness even after becoming a big snake. His dying words are as follows: "Well, gosh."[5]

The unwillingly transformed find themselves much closer to the werewolf mark, from Gregor Samsa's bug transformation in Kafka's *Metamorphosis* to Bottom's jackass conversion in Shakespeare's *A Midsummer Night's Dream*, who courts the fairy queen and observes quite rightly that "reason and love keep little company together nowadays."[6] And we find here as well Guy Mann from *The X-Files*, the horned-toad hominid who gets bitten by a person and then intermittently becomes one. A comic reversal of the wolf curse, that is, the suburbanite curse, whereby Guy gets trapped in various creature discomforts: neckties, alarm clocks, cell phones, resumes. He learns to lie about his love life, too, making the transformation complete, but like Gregor and Bottom, Guy preserves that unique kind of self-consciousness reserved only for people, even if depressed, or foolish, or fooled.[7] The same cannot be said of the werewolf, insofar as the human has been so deeply buried under the wolf pelt that we cannot find the man who was there.

5. Whedon, "Graduation Day, Part 2," season 3, episode 22.

6. Shakespeare, *Midsummer Night's Dream*, 3.1.130–31.

7. Carter, "Mulder and Scully Meet the Were-Monster," season 10, episode 3.

When fighting monsters, one must be careful not to become a monster, Nietzsche once observed, perhaps as a direct consequence of his own fights with monsters.[8] Maybe he had in mind, too, the old Norse lore of the berserker, that fierce bear or wolf warrior who was said to lose all sense of human perspective as he charged headfirst into battle. As if he became something else entirely. To attempt to reason with a berserker is to misunderstand the circumstance, and so, too, the werewolf. We can no more negotiate with werewolves than we can with Melville's preternatural whale.

And speaking of ships at sea, the best of all settings for a werewolf tale may come by way of the *Kolchak* episode aptly titled "The Werewolf." Here, the afflicted man—Bernard Stieglitz—takes a singles cruise on a huge ocean liner and predictably finds himself at home, at least in werewolf form. Only the silver buttons on the captain's dress uniform stand between the beast and absolute carnage. Fortunately, however, a former priest turned cruiser remembers a few words of Latin and enchants the silver, which Kolchak then blasts into the monster, who then falls into the sea. A Rube Goldberg series of events, but no matter. The salient details are these: (1) the holidaymakers got more than they bargained for, not in a good way, and (2) the werewolf looked fantastic in his 1970s-style polyester disco suit.[9]

And though we cannot negotiate with werewolves, we are nevertheless commanded to love them. "Love your neighbor as yourself," Christ declares, paraphrasing Leviticus 19:18, even if your neighbor is a werewolf, presumably. But how to love werewolves is the question, and on this point we might turn for inspiration to the story of Jesus and the demoniac in Mark 5, or Paul and the possessed girl from Acts 16. Curing the possessed is not to argue with theologians but rather to cast out devils. Not that these demonic characters in Scripture are werewolves, exactly, but they participate in the same dark magic that animates the monster. To think otherwise is to misunderstand Leviticus 19:17, which is less

8. Nietzsche, *Beyond Good and Evil*, 89.

9. Rice, "Werewolf," episode 5.

often quoted than Leviticus 19:18: "Rebuke your neighbor frankly so you will not share in their guilt."

We might also study Remus Lupin, if trying to understand our neighbors. The Potterverse's most unwilling of werewolves, he takes great pains to protect himself and others from his affliction, while his diabolical counterpart, Fenrir Greyback, takes no pains whatsoever and instead seeks to indoctrinate all in the way of the wolf. Read symbolically, Greyback is the quintessential apostle of perdition, the drug dealer, the drug fiend, the drowning spiritual swimmer toward whom we must behave knowingly, lest we find ourselves dragged down with him—plummeting together into the abyss.

Goya would have us believe that the sleep of reason is to blame for all this horror, per his masterpiece *The Sleep of Reason Produces Monsters*, but it seems not to be so simple. We might just as easily observe that the sleep of laughter produces monsters, or the sleep of love. And, after all, the presence of reason alone guarantees very little in life. Jonathan Swift's narrator from *A Modest Proposal* is full of casuistic brainpower, and yet concludes by the precepts of his own tight logic that eating children is the best course of action. Along similar lines, the narrator from Poe's "Tell-Tale Heart" is not morbid because he is poetical but rather because he is especially analytical.[10] That said, nobody will accuse the werewolf of being reasonable. Cunning, yes, and full of animal guile, but the point is that an absence of reason itself in no way explains the madness. Some sort of positive evil must be posited, something very much beyond the cunning we see in nature, which is motivated by natural hunger. On the contrary, something wicked animates the wolfman's paranormal hunger.

Exactly where Daniel 4's King Nebuchadnezzar fits into these schemata remains unclear. He lived like an animal for seven years, and had "the mind of an animal," we are told. He ate grass and roamed the open range, but we hear no word of cattle mutilations or missing children, and so the wolf is not a part of the equation, at least not immediately. Some commentators speculate

10. Chesterton, *Orthodoxy*, 8.

that Nebuchadnezzar became a cow, but William Blake's famous depiction suggests otherwise and hits closer to the mark: here, in watercolor, the fallen king looks like a wounded dog, derelict, disheveled, with vacant eyes and the demeanor of a creature in retreat, though still quite dangerous. Had he stayed in the wild for a few more years, then livestock would have likely gone missing, and then—just as likely—people.

With Nebuchadnezzar, Blake provides a visual-rhetorical emblem for how a person becomes a predator, and more than one critic has rightly noticed the striking similarity between Blake's depiction and Lucas Cranach the Elder's 1512 woodcut titled "The Werewolf." The two men are posed similarly, especially at the foot, though in the latter we discover human carnage everywhere. Legs, a detached head, entrails. Cranach's man-wolf also carries in his mouth a small child, leaving the implication unmistakable: werewolf as cannibal; werewolf as child predator. That his monster looks more like a man than a wolf, too, adds a layer of discomfort to the scene, reinforcing one of the woodcut's pronounced moral lessons: appearances deceive. As the apostle Matthew advises, "Beware of the wolf in sheep's clothing."[11]

These same connotations of cannibalism and child abuse accompany most of the werewolf tales down through the centuries, from *Little Red Riding Hood* to the late medieval folklore of Jewish werewolves who lived on the edges of European towns, stole children, and performed gruesome rituals under the light of the full moon.[12] So the propaganda tells us. The female witch ultimately defeated the male werewolf in the battle for primacy as Renaissance Europe's most sinister emblem of demonic inversion, and early America's, too, but the werewolf has always persisted, reminding the naïve Rousseauians among us that we find ourselves always just one metonym away from monstrosity.

The caveat, of course, is that the terror of the werewolf is never the wolf itself, which has been hunted to extinction in certain parts of the world, sadly. The terror instead is that of spiritual bestiality,

11. Matthew 7:15.

12. Shyovitz, "Twelfth-Century Werewolf Renaissance," 521–43.

the corruption of the human soul through some form of unholy magic. Not the curse of Adam, precisely, though the Fall obviously precedes the problem, but some adjacent consequence, the curse of the sons of God per Genesis 6, for example, who gave rise to a thousand shadowy chimeras, among them the werewolves.

If we are to find the werewolf more fully realized in Scripture, then we should turn to Acts 19 in the New Testament and Judges 19 in the Old. In the former, seven Jewish exorcists enter a small house where a possessed man dwells. Possessed by what kind of demon, exactly, we do not know, but we have one good clue. Moments after entering, they flee in terror and, more to the point, naked. What could have so easily disrobed them? And why? Some critics speculate that the nakedness is to be read in a purely symbolic fashion, signaling the bones beneath whitewashed tombs.[13] No hint of sexual intercourse need be involved, they say, but for those who have been in the company of seven unexpectedly naked men in a small house, the purely symbolic seldom applies. Perhaps the story's most prescient detail is this: they preferred to be exposed in public rather than concealed in a small room with a particular type of devil. Who could blame them?

More overtly connected to werewolf lore, and more troublingly so, is the bizarre episode in Judges 19—on which pastors have delivered very few sermons.[14] Here, a Levite's concubine meets a horrible fate at the hands of the Benjamites, to whom Scripture refers as ravenous wolves. The Levite and his concubine take refuge in a gracious stranger's house, we might recall, at which point the evil Benjamites pound on the door and demand that the homeowner deliver to them the Levite so that he might be repeatedly raped. Instead, however, the owner offers to them his virgin daughter and the concubine, which should strike any sensible ear—in any era—as an astonishingly inappropriate gesture. Tragically, the men deliver the concubine into the hands of the evildoers, sparing the virgin daughter, and what happens next is predictable. We discover the concubine—in the morning—dead

13. Matthew 23:27.

14. Sterne, "Levite and His Concubine," 167–76.

on the porch, having obviously been abused all night. Who could have done this, if not men transmogrified into beasts? Who would behave in this way, if not werewolves?

Critics rightly connect the bronze serpent in Numbers 21 to Christ, by virtue of the allusion to it in John 3:14–15: "And as Moses lifted up the serpent in the wilderness, so must the Son of Man be lifted up, that whoever believes in him may have eternal life." Fewer critics connect the Levite's concubine to Christ, but they should. She certainly prefigures Christ's death at the hands of a wolfish world, and perhaps also his resurrection, oddly, if we connect the bizarre act of her dismemberment later in chapter 19 to the logic of Osiris, the murdered Egyptian god whose body fragments portended fertility as the priests and birds scattered them throughout the land, only to be reassembled in the springtime.

But no matter how often the world's fragments are scattered and then reassembled, they do not fall into the shapes of werewolves, at least not normally, nor into the shapes of basilisks: that is, the serpent-rooster hybrid. Such is Plato's critique of the atomists, who fail to appreciate the transcendental forms behind material reality.[15] And in defense of Plato, we have no herds, or dens, or congregations of basilisks, but this need not mean that the beast proves impossible. What Plato overlooks is the magic done by moonlight, spells of the sort Lucius Apuleius wields to a ridiculous consequence in *Metamorphosis*, where he inadvertently turns himself into a jackass.[16] Or, in the opposite direction, spells cast by the old Roman priesthood, who turn bread and wine into flesh and blood. This is the magic of transmutation, for better or worse, and worse, still, by the sorcery of the werewolf malediction.

In the old country, werewolves in the collective were not called "packs" or "routes" but rather "bondages," a term that makes explicit how the wolf curse imprisons the psyche. But as the biblical writers tell us, the world will not always be like this. At some point, the world will change, and all who have thorns in their sides will find comfort. And all who have thorns in their paws—the same.

15. Plato, *Laws*, 359.

16. Apuleius, *Metamorphoses*, 3.137.

A final thought: among the often misremembered Bible verses is Isaiah 11:6, where many have it that the lion and the lamb lie down together. In point of fact, it is the wolf and lamb. They are to be reconciled, and the passage holds more intrigue as well:

> The wolf will live with the lamb,
> the leopard will lie down with the goat,
> the calf and the lion and the yearling together;
> and a little child will lead them.
> The cow will feed with the bear,
> their young will lie down together,
> and the lion will eat straw like the ox.
> The infant will play near the cobra's den,
> and the young child will put its hand into the viper's nest.
> They will neither harm nor destroy
> on all my holy mountain,
> for the earth will be filled
> with the knowledge of the Lord
> as the waters cover the sea.

And on some future judgment day when all is set right, we might also find the concubine from Judges 19, who dances on the bright Plutonian shoreline, splashing water in the air. Maybe she laughs because she cannot help it, and blows kisses to her one true love.

3

Zombies

The Christian and the Materialist hold
different beliefs about the universe.

—*C. S. Lewis*

A ZOMBIE IS A CORPSE reanimated by some type of sorcery. This is the classic definition. Old Europe calls the creature a "revenant," but the same idea holds. Modern zombies, however, are often caused by other means. In George Romero's *Night of the Living Dead*, for example, radiation from the planet Venus animates the corpses, and in *Zombieland*—a virus from the government. Same with *Shaun of the Dead*, *The Walking Dead*, and *Warm Bodies*, which prompts a timely caveat: there are zombies and then "zombies," not all of which are paranormal.

On how Frankenstein's monster came to life, nobody knows for sure, but he is more urbane than zombies tend to be.[1] Nor do Jewish golems and Frosty the Snowman count. The latter sings too much, and both are wrongly formulated. Frosty comes from snow,

1. Brooks, *Young Frankenstein*.

obviously, and the golems from mere loam, not what the Renaissance playwrights call "gilded loam," that is, already pre-assembled bodies, which is a zombie requirement.[2] Tolkien's orcs function likewise as golem-esque monsters, cast from miry clay and then enlivened by the grim magic of Mordor. We do not, for instance, discover scenes with orc children.

And neither is Pinocchio a zombie, nor Pris from *Blade Runner*, but dolls, automatons, and C3POs border upon the land of zombies insofar as they all carry a non-human tint. Zombies, however, carry something else as well, a history of personhood, and so in their present form appear as macabre parodies of the human condition writ large. They are gruesome undead doppelgangers, reminding us of who we are not and perhaps—too—of where we are not. Hell is a place prepared for the Devil and his angels, Christ tells us in Matthew 25:41. And maybe, subsequently, for zombies.

Kolchak, in an episode of *Kolchak: The Night Stalker* aptly titled "The Zombie," correctly discerns the grim scenario at hand: "He, sir, is from Hell itself!"[3] C. S. Lewis pursues a similar line of thinking in *The Problem of Pain*:

> You will remember that in the parable, the saved go to a place prepared for them, while the damned go to a place never made for men at all. To enter Heaven is to become more human than you ever succeeded in being on earth; to enter Hell is to be banished from humanity. What is cast (or casts itself) into Hell is not a man: it is "remains."[4]

Lewis makes an intriguing point, which has as its crescendo the now-famous line about the doors of Hell: "I willingly believe that the damned are, in one sense, successful, rebels to the end; that the doors of Hell are locked on the inside by zombies."[5] I added the last part about zombies, of course, but only in an effort to illustrate the

2. Shakespeare, *Richard II*, 1.1.179.
3. Rice, "Zombie," episode 2.
4. Lewis, *Problem of Pain*, 128.
5. Lewis, *Problem of Pain*, 130.

ontological crux of Lewis's argument: there are no people as such in Hell.

But if not, then what about that eerie episode in Luke 16? Here, we find the tale of the rich man and the beggar, the former of whom is parched because he sits in flames. He sees Abraham across the great divide, and the beggar Lazarus, too, and asks Abraham to let Lazarus bring him water. Additional details prove unnecessary, except to say that the rich man finds himself in Hell and yet appears to have his faculties intact, as if still human. Or mostly human. How can this be, if there are no people as such in Hell? The short answer—I think—goes something like this: the rich man has achieved his goal. Under the circumstances, this is a reasonable explanation, though we do well to amplify the point by invoking 1 Corinthians 10:21: we are free to drink when we drink, but if so, then we are not free to still be dry.[6] Put differently, the rich man is where he wants to be, guarding his treasure, and until this changes, there he will be—even if he protests to the contrary. The caution, however, is that he will surrender the ability to protest at some point, one presumes, and then begin to resemble more clearly a zombie who sits on a pile of gold.

Not everyone believes in Hell, needless to say, yet most concede that some people behave worse than others, which also helps our cause.[7] Indeed, part of zombie lore's wisdom is to show that bad people often produce more horror than the zombies themselves. Such is the character of Legendre Murder, a case in point from the film *White Zombie*. Not fortunate in name, Mr. Murder runs "a dark Satanic mill" populated by hordes of zombie workers, which is the film's heavy-handed critique of sociopathic industrialization.[8] The truth to be gleaned, here, is that zombies did not invent the multinational corporation; rather, they fell prey to it.

We might think, too, of Herman Melville's dehumanized characters from *Bartleby the Scrivener*: Nippers, Turkey, Ginger Nut, and the other functionaries whose nicknames themselves indicate

6. Lewis, *Great Divorce*, 41.

7. Sartre, *No Exit*, 45.

8. Halperin, *White Zombie*; Blake, *Poems*, 207.

the functions. From an economic standpoint, their value becomes a matter of utility, not essence, which is Melville's reproach of the despairingly corporate drive to objectify personhood—of which zombies are an example beyond the pale. They might as well be fleshy mannequins, in fact, and as such provide the perfect foil for the human being properly conceived.

Here, then, is why we do not blame zombies for eating brains, nor do we hold them accountable for wearing white pants after Labor Day, as some inevitably do. They cannot help it—in ethics and in fashion. Perhaps especially in fashion. The best we can hope for in the realm of zombie couture is Solomon Grundy, the quasi-zombie supervillain who holds up his frayed pants with a frayed rope, a fashion victory to be sure, however small it might be, though "zombie fashion" is a misnomer in the final analysis. They wear clothes, but not for the same reasons we do.

The point holds true for Salvador Dali's zombies as well, most of whom find themselves in nice dresses. I make this point—in part—to correct those in the cognoscenti who dismiss zombies as a subject too lowbrow for serious consideration. Not so. Exhibit A: the avant-garde Dali, darling of the highbrow, or at least still of the middlebrow, now that his paintings appear on T-shirts and coffee mugs. *Burning Giraffe. Mirage. Woman with Head of Roses.* All zombies, too ramshackle and emaciated to live, never mind the missing head on the last one, and yet there they are posed for the leering eye, not unlike those heroin-chic supermodels from *Vogue* magazine in the late 1990s. Necrophilia never looked so stylish.

But never let it be said that zombies are lazy. They are tired, to be sure. Their ragged countenances tell us this, but they are not indolent. Zombies live purpose-driven undead lives. They want to eat brains, or any human flesh, depending on the mythos, and their calendars are organized accordingly. No naps. No swimming lessons. Just brains. But we quickly discern that no amount of flesh will satisfy. There is always one more hapless minimart clerk to ambush, one more sorority girl in bunny slippers to chase down the corridor. In this way, the zombie's gloomy predicament bears a striking resemblance to that of the Danaids in the classical underworld, those sisters condemned to fill a sieve with water for all eternity, an emblem of the perverse appetite unchecked, which has at its core the irony of insatiable hunger. And as the pleasure becomes less and less, the craving becomes more and more. The law of diminishing returns. So it is with all vices. The love of money demands more money, and the love of brains, more brains.

The love of Machiavellian intrigue, however, is a different matter entirely. Zombies do not find themselves arrested for money laundering schemes, for example, nor do they engage in passive-aggressive office politics. In fact, zombies wear their hearts on their sleeves, sometimes literally, and leave little doubt about their motivation, which is to say that zombies carry with them an almost child-like transparency. "Motive" is likely the wrong word to use in such cases, because what they do is born largely out of muscle memory, at least in terms of the physical logistics. We find this point amusingly illustrated in a *Z Nation* episode titled "The Collector," where zombie George R. R. Martin—played by Martin himself—sits chained to a desk and signs books out of sheer habit.[9] The episode's antagonist, The Collector, believes the books to be valuable and imagines selling them in a post-apocalyptic bookstore, once the zombie dust settles. But would they sell, even if the Collector had such a bookstore? And, more to the point, would they sell as authentically signed books?

In philosophy of mind, this area of inquiry is called "the zombie problem," wherein philosophers postulate differences between people and zombies, all for the sake of determining what one believes human consciousness to be. For behaviorists in the tradition of B. F. Skinner, and for other functionalists and rote materialists, too, there is no categorical distinction. By the logic of such worldviews, humans are—for all practical purposes—fleshy robots, some with more intact mechanisms than others.[10] On the contrary, the spiritualist, the Baptist, the panpsychic idealist, and so on, will find troubling the behaviorist's failure to account for

9. Schaefer and Engler, "Collector," season 2, episode 8.

10. Kirk, "Zombies."

self-awareness and the qualia contained therein.[11] Such elements of the inner life should not exist if the spokes and gears of physicalism are true, and yet they do exist in plain sight, for all to see, as if to say that physicalism refutes itself to the extent that it participates in its own self-consciousness.[12]

Still, the typical physicalist will declare that George R. R. Martin signed the book if zombie Martin signed it, but for the typical transcendental philosopher, zombie Martin's signature proves suspect at best, mainly on the ground that zombies are more like robots than people, the latter of whom are comprised of flesh, to be sure, but also starlight and magic—both of which are implied in a live signature.

Mary Shelley understood the point, which is why The Modern Prometheus reads Albertus Magnus, Cornelius Agrippa, and Paracelsus, the esoteric alchemist, all in preparation for the sorcery to come.[13] And Shelley, too, studied these authors, along with her father William Godwin's *Lives of the Necromancers*, the recurring motif of which is that one requires more than science to enliven the dead. And even when enlivened, the dead are not who we might expect them to be. The night's Plutonian shore changes people, usually for the worse, a lesson inherent in every honest book of necromancy ever written.

We arrive therefore, inevitably, at the persistent argument that Christ himself is a zombie, correctly understood, an idea to which the cynics seem especially happy to subscribe. In response, religious philosophers do well to say that the likelihood of Christ being a zombie is the same as the likelihood of Christ being a great moral teacher. Jesus claims to be the Son of God, at much peril, sent to reconcile the world to himself, which is either true or evidence of a particularly deluded man. Or, worse still, evidence of a charlatan. In light of our conversation, we might therefore revisit Lewis's trilemma and add a fourth possibility. A quadrilemma: Jesus as

11. Jackson, "What Mary Didn't Know," 291–95.

12. Dickerson, *Mind and the Machine*, 24.

13. Shelley, *Frankenstein*, 29.

lunatic, liar, Lord, or zombie.[14] Regardless, the great-moral-teacher argument goes out the window. His claims are too transformational to fit within moral frameworks ordinarily understood. His claims are too disturbing to be taken as great moral teachings, unless—of course—he is who he says he is.

And so, in conclusion, a prayer. God bless the obsessive-compulsive internet shoppers, the warehouse workers on unnecessarily tight schedules, and the machine-like managers of the big data algorithms. God bless the students who sedate themselves in order to survive their own educations, taking standardized test after standardized test. And God bless the Emily Griersons of the world, who keep their petrified-boyfriend corpses near them in the bedroom, an emblem of what happens when one tries too mightily to hold on to the past.[15] And God help us, too, when we see in our own reflections a zombie-like affectation, the abyss who stares back at us and falsely claims that we are not the righteousness of God, as Paul says we are in 2 Corinthians 5:21. And, finally, Godspeed to Gussie Fink-Nottle from the P. G. Wodehouse sagas: "Many an experienced undertaker would have been deceived by his appearance, and started embalming on sight."[16]

14. Lewis, *Mere Christianity*, 52.

15. Faulkner, "Rose for Emily," 59.

16. Wodehouse, *Right Ho, Jeeves*, 46.

4

Ghosts

Our forefathers looked upon nature with more reverence and horror before the world was enlightened by learning and philosophy, and loved to astonish themselves with the apprehensions of witchcraft, prodigies, charms, and enchantments. There was not a village in England that had not a ghost in it, the church-yards were all haunted, every large common had a circle of fairies belonging to it, and there was scarce a shepherd who had not seen a spirit.

—*Joseph Addison*

Nature is a haunted house.

—*Emily Dickinson*

MOMENTS BEFORE RIP VAN Winkle falls asleep for twenty years, he drinks enchanted liquor and plays ninepins with the ghost Henry Hudson and his lost crew of sailors. The scene precedes *The Big Lebowski* by nearly two centuries. Rip stumbles upon the phantoms high in the Catskill mountains, in a well-hidden hollow lit by shards of moonlight through the canopy. It is a gothic-comic setting, made all the more comical by Rip's willingness to barrel headlong into the party, as if he has no reason to be wary. But we are wary for him, as is Wolf, his dog, who growls like dogs do when they detect preternatural energies.[1] We are also wary because the apparitions carry on their faces otherworldly and purgatorial expressions, despite the bowling, despite the drinking, and they wear antique Dutch clothing, including puffy pantaloons, which eliminates the possibility that they are fairies, who would not be caught dead or alive in such a fashion travesty. We arrive, then, at the first two of several pressing questions about ghosts: out of what are their pants made and, perhaps more to the point, out of what are they made?

Ghosts seem not to age, nor do their clothes. Whatever material reality they possess, or assemble when they manifest themselves, something about ghost magic functions in a different temporal mode. They are out of normal time and yet obviously capable of temporal interactions, much like René Magritte's *Modern Venus*, for example, whom we discover at that halfway point between Heaven and Earth, the archetype and the incarnation. On the contrary, when Rip wakes up twenty-years later, his pants are in ruins, and his shoes. His face—wrinkled; his beard—even longer. But Hudson and his crew, wherever they have gone, presumably look the same.

And so, too, does the Ghost of Christmas Future from Charles Dickens's *A Christmas Carol*. He has worn that same black hoodie since the beginning of Christmas, and will until the end, when God wipes away the tears and death shall be no more.[2] But the Ghost of Christmas Past provides an exception to the general rule that apparitions always look the same. The ghost wears a glittery, bedazzled belt which does not change, but underneath the belt he fluctuates, "being now a thing with one arm, now with one leg, now with twenty legs, now a pair of legs without a head, now a head without a body: of which dissolving parts, no outline would

1. Irving, *Rip van Winkle*, 13.

2. Revelation 21:4.

be visible in the dense gloom wherein they melted away."[3] In other words, the past is malleable; it is a Rorschach-style apparition: oscillating, chimerical. We persistently accommodate our past to the present, both of which slip away as time marches on.

"Who controls the past controls the future," George Orwell once observed, and "who controls the present controls the past."[4] This is good and well. Orwell rightly warns us against those who would control the present at all cost, the totalitarians, but his observation brings with it a recalcitrant fact to which Orwell himself may not have been entirely privy: ghosts are inordinately difficult to control. Tyrants fear them.

Macbeth discovers this fact in a most untimely manner. Surrounded by allies, having murdered the king and Banquo, Macbeth stands horrified as Banquo's ghost arrives unannounced and certainly uninvited.[5] Or arrives at least in Macbeth's troubled imagination, if not the world itself. The ghost might be closer in nature to the sound of the tell-tale heart, as Edgar Allan Poe has it, than to a public reality, or closer to the conscience disturbed and then projected, as Daniel Defoe describes in his neglected *History and Reality of Apparitions*:

> Conscience raises many a devil that all the magic in the world can't lay; it shows us many an apparition that no other eyes can see, and sets specters before us with which the Devil has no acquaintance; conscience makes ghosts walk, and departed souls appear, when the souls themselves know nothing of it.[6]

Perhaps Banquo's ghost is of the same order, yet a good argument might be made to the contrary, with the caveat that some ghosts require for their detection a particular type of sensitivity born out of existential angst: murderers, for instance, detect the murdered

3. Dickens, *Christmas Carol*, 27.
4. Orwell, *1984*, 31.
5. Shakespeare, *Macbeth*, 3.4.39–41.
6. Defoe, *History and Reality of Apparitions*, 120.

more acutely than do others, while lovers detect the beloved more acutely as well.

Maybe it goes without saying, also, that we speak here of living ghosts, not those of the holographic or pre-recorded sort. Such ghosts as the latter are possible, of course, and perhaps even common for those who see connections between specters and old Hollywood movies projected onto the big screen. Greta Garbo. Gloria Swanson. Florence Lee. The lore surrounding the haunted Stanley Hotel, too, has it that the nearby mountains function as gigantic natural camcorders, capturing images and then—through the alchemy of orbit and moonlight—projecting them into the building below, often to the sheer terror of the patrons.[7] We should not be skeptical of such possibilities, but these are not the ghosts for whom we look. We look instead for the sentient ghost, the apparition with willpower, the ghost who interacts.

And the disembodied hand of the ghost who interacts, as in the case of Daniel 5. It is the sort of episode one expects to find in Horace Walpole's gothic novels. As the tale goes, a disembodied hand appears out of thin air and writes an inscription on King Belshazzar's palace wall, which Daniel—the master of the magicians—loosely translates as follows: "Not good." Attached to the hand is nothing, and in this way the biblical scene prefigures that moment in *Twin Peaks* where Major Briggs's disembodied head floats through space and whispers "Blue Rose" to Agent Cooper, which is a code phrase to say that something weird goes on, as if a disembodied talking head did not by itself already signal the weirdness.[8]

Much of the rabbinical literature connects the hand in Daniel to the angel Gabriel, the chief messenger among the angels and a key figure in the book of Tobit, which is likely correct, but the deduction is by no means certain. The ghostly father of a wronged peasant girl seems also well within the realm of possibility, especially if he has on his lips Obadiah 1:4: "Though thou exalt thyself

7. Stanley Kubrick filmed *The Shining* here.

8. Lynch, "Call for Help," part 3.

as the eagle, and though thou set thy nest among the stars, thence will I bring thee down, saith the Lord."

Of course, there are more obvious ghost references in Scripture, if our aim is to find such references. Most famously, Saul talks to Samuel's apparition in 1 Samuel 28, when the Witch of Endor summons the prophet and, to her surprise, succeeds. One gets the impression that she expected a familiar spirit, not a ghost. But the real ghost arrives very much intact and proceeds to chide Saul, who has no doubt whatsoever that Samuel is the chider, however ill-advised the conversation happens to be. In fact, the Old Testament holds several admonitions against communions with the dead, which presumably confirm that such communions are possible, if not common.[9] Why warn people otherwise?

In Matthew 14:26, the disciples mistake Christ for a ghost when they see him walk on water: "'It is a ghost,' they say, and are terrified." An understandable mistake, given that people usually sink in such cases. The point to be stressed for our purpose, however, is not the defiance of physics itself, but rather the disciples' explanation for it. The paranormal comes quickly to mind. The ghost thesis is close at hand, and that Christ accepts it as a real possibility should not go unnoticed, which is why he reassures Peter that he is himself, truly, and not a phantasmagorical Jesus doppelgänger. From this episode we might therefore reasonably deduce two things: (1) when a man walks on water, we say "miracle," and (2) when a ghost does the same, we say "yes, it happens." Everybody knows that ghosts can walk on water.

We find a similar scene in Luke 24, where Christ—in an almost comical fashion—explains to the disciples that he is not a ghost. One wonders if this was his default post-resurrection announcement: "I'm not a ghost." He shows the disciples his hands and feet, but they remain incredulous, at which point he eats a piece of boiled fish and thus settles a long-standing debate within paranormal research circles: ghosts do not eat boiled fish.

What is saved is not a ghost, C. S. Lewis reminds us in "The Weight of Glory" and illustrates in *The Great Divorce*, where ethereal

9. Deuteronomy 18:9–12; Leviticus 19:31; Isaiah 8:19.

spirits populate Hell, not Heaven.[10] Some are preacher ghosts. On occasion, they fly up to shallow Paradise and, with bat-like voices, minister to the saved—imploring them to shake off the fetters of their bondage and join the real utopia below.[11] Like the sophist Belial, they try to make the worse appear the better reason. Misery loves company. Other ghosts fly back to earth and visit old haunts. Some go to college libraries, hoping to see their books in the hands of students. Others return to give terrible advice to young men, which is the supernatural setting of Shakespeare's *Hamlet*.

Or was King Hamlet's ghost a ghost at all? Exactly how to distinguish between the dead and the demonic is an always-timely question, with the hallucinatory realm constituting a third way still. We are "to test the spirits," as the author of 1 John 4:1 entreats us to do, "to see whether they are from God." And if not, then from whom? Such is *Hamlet*'s crux, a ghost story, where our protagonist spends much of the play mulling over the nature of the apparition with whom he comes into contact: this "thing," "this dreaded sight," an "illusion," a "spirit of health or goblin damned."[12] Because Horatio and others also see the phantom, critics are quick to dismiss the hallucination thesis, and understandably so, though there is a psychosis called "folie à deux," the madness of two, or the madness of many, whereby groups hallucinate assorted phenomena. *Hamlet*, however, is almost certainly not one of those times, and neither was that infamous performance of *Faustus*, I suspect, on the night when two devils took to the stage simultaneously, one acting and the other not, which sent the audience scrambling for the doors.[13]

"Of all the particulars in which the modern stage falls short of the ancient," Henry Fielding observes in eighteenth-century England, "there is none so much to be lamented, as the great scarcity of ghosts in the latter."[14] To this end, to the remedy of the lament,

10. Lewis, "Weight of Glory," 14.

11. Lewis, *Great Divorce*, 80.

12. Shakespeare, *Hamlet*, 1.4.40.

13. Thomas, *Religion and the Decline of Magic*, 230.

14. Fielding, *Tragedy of Tragedies*, 83.

Fielding writes two of the funniest ghost scenes in the Western canon. First is a moment in *Tom Thumb* when our Lilliputian hero returns from the grave—having been eaten by a large cow on main street. In ghost form now, Tom declares himself to be invincible, only to be easily killed a second time by the character Grizzle, in an episode famous for causing the overly grave Jonathan Swift to laugh out loud in public.[15] Second is the scene in the play's sequel, *Tragedy of Tragedies*, where Tom's father—Gaffer—appears as the ghost of record, mainly to parody the king's ghost from *Hamlet*. He uses mock-ominous language and makes annoying noises at midnight in the kitchen: "Ye fairies, goblins, bats, and screech-owls, hail," he says, all the while banging pots and pans and searching for gin. When King Arthur understandably threatens to kill him if he does not quiet down, Gaffer drolly replies, "I am a ghost, and I am already dead," which amuses those of us who remember Tom's double death in the play's previous incarnation.[16]

A ghost is the soul of tragedy, Aristotle declares in the *Poetics*, which might be another way of saying that nostalgia pricks us all.[17] We are not made for this world, at least not exactly, and the ghost reminds us of this, but apparitions are signposts of the divine comedy as well, insofar as they reassure us that death is not the end, and, too, that the world is full of strange energy. As Hamlet famously says, and Major Briggs not-so-famously repeats to Agent Cooper in *Twin Peaks*, "There are more things in heaven and earth, Horatio, than are dreamt of in your philosophy."[18]

So, naturally, we wonder where ghosts reside when they do not reside with us. Maybe Purgatory, but such a term will bother the Protestants, at which point the phrase "Protestant Purgatory" might be helpful. The Jews have Abraham's Bosom, a material place for the righteous dead who await the Messiah in peace and quiet. Buddhists will talk of the Bardo, a liminal state between death and

15. Fielding, *Tom Thumb*, 2.4.11.

16. Fielding, *Tragedy of Tragedies*, 3.2.10.

17. Cited in Fielding, *Tragedy of Tragedies*, 83.

18. Shakespeare, *Hamlet*, 1.5.167–68; Lynch, "Arbitrary Law," season 2, episode 9.

rebirth, while other traditions will have other phrases for similar ideas. In a dangerously poetic image, Plato gives us the dead who drink from Lethe's waters and then return to the world—transmigrated. In Homer's underworld all are ghosts, happy or not. Ghost Sisyphus rolls his rock, and phantom Tantalus reaches toward—but never quite touches—the phantom apple. Same with the Roman underworld, where Aeneas meets Dido and weeps, aware that their roles have been reversed, that she is now the stoic, and he the tender-hearted lover.[19] As a young man, Augustine cried over this scene, but later recanted the tears on the premise that Christians should not be moved by pagan literature, reluctant—it seems—to acknowledge that all truths are God's truths, pagan or not.[20]

The materialists have Gilbert Ryle, who describes human consciousness itself as "the ghost in the machine," which begs the question of the sentient ghost.[21] The problem, here, is that Ryle imagines consciousness to be an epiphenomenon of the material world, a side effect of material causality. But might not he and his entourage have the world exactly backwards? To cite Chesterton, Max Planck, Rupert Sheldrake, and the author of John 1:1, mind precedes matter.[22] Mind is the precondition from which matter emerges, not the other way around, which is to say that the storyteller precedes the story, just as Luther precedes the Lutheran Reformation, just as disco music precedes disco fashion, for better or oftentimes worse. In the beginning was the Word, and from the Word came the material cosmos.[23]

With Chesterton handy, we might also turn to an analogical argument against the ghost debunkers, of whom there are many: "A false ghost disproves the reality of ghosts," he observes in *Orthodoxy*, "exactly as much as a forged banknote disproves the existence of the Bank of England."[24] If anything, the forged note

19. Virgil, *Aeneid*, 6.443.

20. Augustine, *Confessions*, 14.

21. Cathcart and Klein, *Plato and a Platypus*, 128.

22. Chesterton, *Orthodoxy*, 134; Sheldrake, *Science Set Free*, 212–30.

23. Farmer, *Gospel of John*, 86.

24. Chesterton, *Orthodoxy*, 146.

confirms the reality of banks. Those who experience the globe's many cultures might also marshal an anthropological argument against the debunkers: that is, ghost lore persists in every culture. In every corner of the earth we discover tales of visitations and phantom menaces, stories of disembodied voices, anecdotes of specters in the attic. Not all are credible, needless to say, but those who believe in the ghost realm tend to have evidence, while those who disavow such possibilities usually do so on purely doctrinal grounds. That is, they have doctrines against ghosts, which preemptively nullify all evidence to the contrary. "This cannot be a ghost," the skeptics say of Ghost Rider, for example, "because our philosophy will not allow for it."

On ghosts in general, the skeptics fall short, I believe, but they might have a point with Ghost Rider, of Marvel comic book fame, who seems not to be a ghost proper, but rather a skeleton with a flaming head. He is something closer in nature to the dancing bones in the Valley of the Bones (Ezekiel 37) than to a ghost as such. Nor do ghosts usually ride vintage motorcycles, unless they are ghost motorcycles, which is not the case here. "Perpetually flaming skeleton rider," however, raises more questions than it answers. Plus, we must admit that something ghostly is involved, given that the flame does not consume but only burns. In this way, Ghost Rider may cause us to ponder the rich man in Luke 16 who sits in the fire but is not spent. Or he may be close in metaphysics to the burning bush from Exodus 3:2: "And the angel of the LORD appeared unto him in a flame of fire out of the midst of a bush: and he looked, and, behold, the bush burned with fire, and the bush was not consumed." Not that the Ghost Riders of the world are angels, but they exist nonetheless in that celestial space where materiality can hold flames without dire consequences.

On the contrary, some ghosts seem not to know they are ghosts. They believe themselves to be living in the houses they haunt, to be walking in the fields they once tended. When Ghost Rider looks in the mirror, he knows immediately that the world has changed, but we cannot say the same for Professor Binns, who teaches his classes at Hogwarts per usual, unaware that he died many years ago.[25] Here, then, is J. K. Rowling's wry commentary on those who have long-since abandoned teaching and now simply go through the motions, a morality tale for professors everywhere. Parson Yorick from Sterne's *Sentimental Journey*, too, seems not to understand that he passed away in 1748 as he embarks upon his 1763 journey through France, where he flirts with women and discovers—finally—that Christianity, when rightly practiced, is meekness and candor, love and courtesy.[26] Such is the wisdom of Yorick's final theosis, by which he passes from this world to the next, and from the old body to the new.

And such also was the promise of early Christianity, before the Nicene Creed and the logistics of competing atonement theories. At root, the very early Christians converted on the promise of our resurrection through Christ, which brought with it a new material reality. The New Jerusalem: a place where our bodies can handle all the pleasures of Heaven. We might blush with embarrassment, said the early church fathers, if we could only half-glimpse the physical joys in store for us in the next world.

I recall, now, those memes of ethereal spirits who sit lethargically on clouds, pluck harps, and hold blank expressions on their faces. They are surprised to discover Hell's irony.

Docetism is the doctrine that Christ's flesh was not human at all but rather phantasmagoric, and that his sufferings were therefore only apparent, not real, not embodied. This is the Gnostic heresy, and those who hold to it do so in high regard, because for them the material world is a prison.[27] Women who have babies, therefore, sin cardinally against the canons of Gnosticism, as do those who too much enjoy hot chocolate and the warmth of a crackling fire on a cold October night. By this logic, such comforts prove comfortable only to the unenlightened, they who have not yet transcended the pleasure of the kiss and the joy of holding a baby tightly in one's arms.

25. Rowling, *Harry Potter and the Chamber of Secrets*, 148.

26. Stark, *Biblical Sterne*, 71–92.

27. Swift, "Mechanical Operation of the Spirit," 126–41.

The Gnostics insist that immateriality is a marvelous thing. They dream of pure spirit and dismiss the material coil as a cage. But later in the evening, after the guests have gone home, after the wine, do these same Gnostics slow dance for a moment in their living rooms, alone, and think of lost loves, while ghostly music plays in the background? Maybe something romantic from the big band era? Do they become once more conflicted on the question of embodiment?

5

Robots

For as we think in our hearts, so we are.

—*Proverbs 23:7*

MUCH LORE SURROUNDS THE now-destroyed cross at Boxley monastery, known also as the Rood of Grace. By general consensus the bare facts are these: (1) a mechanical Jesus of some sort hung upon a cross, (2) the Protestants destroyed it in 1538, at the behest of John Hilsey, the Bishop of Rochester, and (3) the puppet moved in response to the pilgrims, some of whom assumed it to be in synchronicity with God Almighty, not the puppeteers.[1] The Protestants may have been righteous iconoclasts, or they may have been grim courtiers, and the degree to which the mechanical Jesus moved also remains a point of disagreement. Some have him nodding and blinking. Some say he wept and bent his shoulders, while others give him a full range of gesticulations, all in service of separating devotees from their money. Or so the cynics contend. As Ambrose Bierce observes in *The Devil's Dictionary*,

1. Groeneveld, "Boxley Rood," 11–50.

rhabdomancers use divining rods to prospect for precious metals in the pockets of fools, and clairvoyants have the power to see that which is invisible to their clients, namely, that they are blockheads.[2]

But playing God is easier said than done. One wonders if the Jesus puppeteers ever imagined themselves to be in over their heads, especially when presented with those most palpable forms of suffering before God: the prayers of the downtrodden, of those who have lost too much already, of parents who scan the horizon—hoping to catch a glimpse of their prodigal sons or daughters who told them they found good work in the city. And the Jesus puppeteers undoubtedly also heard the prayers of Pharisees and publicans per Luke 18: "Two men went up to the temple to pray," Christ tells us, "one a Pharisee and the other a tax collector. The first thanked God that he was not like other people, while the second wisely cried out 'God, have mercy on me, a sinner!'" Did these puppeteers ever cry out similarly as they maneuvered the Jesus puppet?

Jacques de Vaucanson did not build a Jesus machine, but he did invent a set of android butlers designed to clean up after the brothers of the holy order.[3] This happened in eighteenth-century France. The chief monk responded angrily, declaring the mechanical men to be profane, and so with a hammer smashed the droids into a thousand pieces. A similarly violent scene unfolded five centuries earlier when the Dominican friar Albertus Magnus built a brass android—to the horror of Thomas Aquinas. Also in proximity of a hammer, Aquinas obliterated the machine and thus confirmed one of the world's most sensible minor rules of thumb: keep hammers away from theologians.[4]

What then became of Vaucanson? A few years after his debacle with the monks, he was chased out of Lyons by rioting workers with scissors, not hammers, because he contrived a new

2. Bierce, *Devil's Dictionary*, 336, 36.

3. Wood, *Living Dolls*, 17.

4. Wood, *Living Dolls*, xvi.

technology to streamline the production of silk.[5] A job-killing machine. Understandably, the workers' guild took exception.

Later, perhaps having learned his lesson, Vaucanson invented his masterpiece, a mechanical duck notable for its ability to poop.[6] He also invented moving statues that played music, a percussionist and a flautist, specifically, both in homage to the lore of old Rhodes. The island had a garden of moving statues created by Daedalus, as the story goes, which Pindar describes as such:

> The animated figures stand
> Adorning every public street
> And seem to breathe in stone, or
> move their marble feet.[7]

In the *Meno*, Socrates adds a provocative anecdote, suggesting that these ancient automatons needed to be to tied down at night—lest they "play truant and run away."[8] They developed a will of their own, we are lead to believe, and a deep awareness that the pedestal is no place to live. Notably, Vaucanson's statues were bolted to the base as well.

And so too Pygmalion's Galatea, carved into marble and firmly fixed to the pedestal—until Aphrodite freed her. Properly speaking, of course, she was not an android at all, given the absence of an Antikythera mechanism by which her heart kept time, but she certainly acted like something more than a marble statue. Ovid has it that Pygmalion sat with her on the sofa long before she came to life, and always made sure she felt comfortable in her pose. We might therefore place Galatea alongside the golems and tulpas of the old world, and, for that matter, the Pinocchios, who begin their lives as puppets but then, in moments of transcendental wonderment, become real people by virtue of the Blue Fairy's dream magic. Regardless of how we finally describe Galatea, this much should be clear: Pygmalion had no capacity to ensoul her.

5. Wood, *Living Dolls*, 38.
6. Wood, *Living Dolls*, 26–27.
7. Pindar, "Seventh Olympic Ode," 40.
8. Plato, *Meno*, 3.97.

He simply set down the occasion, with the caveat that Aphrodite provided the golden touch.

Hephaestus gave Talos another kind of golden touch entirely. The gargantuan android guarded the island of Crete, hurling boulders at passersby and incinerating boats with the fire that came from his fingers. Fatally, however, Talos tried to kill Jason of Jason-and-the-Argonauts fame, for whom the sorceress Medea felt much affection. Ergo, she hypnotized the dreadful machine (proving that robots can be hypnotized), at which point Talos willingly removed the brass nail from his ankle, the linchpin, all with Medea's promise that to do so would make him human. Instead, as those who know the story know, magic blood flowed from his ankle like rocket fuel, and his life force ebbed away, leaving Talos where he started long ago—that is—a cumbersome piece of metal. Ashes to ashes, adamantium to adamantium.

Do not take down a fence until you know why it was put up, the wise philosophers say, and something similar might be said of linchpins and the pulling out thereof.[9] More generally speaking, attractive sorcerers and advertising executives alike seldom have altruistic motives in mind when they ask us reconfigure ourselves with promises of utopia in the offing. Such is the nature of all Faustian bargains.

The moral of the Talos story remains a matter of dispute, but those who feel sympathy for the robot often invoke—at some point during the apology—Roy Batty's speech from *Blade Runner*, which carries with it an almost boyish innocence:

> I've seen things you people wouldn't believe. Attack ships on fire off the shoulder of Orion. I watched C-beams glitter in the dark near the Tannhäuser Gate. All those moments will be lost in time, like tears in rain.[10]

Here is an android's knowing lament, as earnest as can be, and more earnest in mood than the language of several humans with whom we come into contact in the film, confirming that people at

9. Chesterton, *Why I Am a Catholic*, 160.

10. Scott, *Blade Runner*.

times make themselves too difficult to distinguish from machines. Perhaps the real danger in robotics is not that humanoid robots will be difficult to recognize as machines, but rather that some people will be difficult to recognize as people because they will too much emulate rote machinery. As Marshall McLuhan observes, "we become what we behold."[11]

Darwin understood the point as well, when, near the end of his career, and upon realizing that he no longer enjoyed poetry, painting, music, and Shakespeare, confessed the following:

> My mind seems to have become a kind of machine for grinding general laws out of large collections of facts, but why this should have caused the atrophy of that part of the brain alone, on which the higher tastes depend, I cannot conceive.[12]

Of Shakespeare, in particular, he spoke the harshest: "I have tried lately to read Shakespeare, and found it so intolerably dull that it nauseated me."[13] *Hamlet* is a tragedy, and *King Lear*, also, but so too is the man who finds them dull. And of the world's men who should not be trusted, near the front of the line stand those who cannot laugh at the great one-liners in *Much Ado about Nothing*: "I would my horse had the speed of your tongue"; "I had rather hear my dog bark at a crow than a man swear he loves me."[14]

There is a small point to be corrected in Roy Batty's magnificent speech on time and rain, incidentally, if we might return to that speech for a moment. Namely, Roy misunderstands the status of all those moments in time, which he believes will be lost. They will not. God knows when the sparrow falls from the sky, and counts every hair on every head, and notices every tear from every eye, even those in the rain.[15]

11. McLuhan, *Understanding Media*, 45.
12. Darwin, *Autobiography*, 139.
13. Darwin, *Autobiography*, 138.
14. Shakespeare, *Much Ado about Nothing*, 1.1.140, 1.1.131–32.
15. Matthew 10:29–30.

Nor will Zhora's tears be lost, the robot prostitute in *Blade Runner* who, when told by Detective Decker that she might be surprised to hear that some men act badly behind closed doors, responds, "No, I wouldn't."[16] If ever a robot understood, then it is here. And when she dies in the department store, lacerated, bleeding on the floor, cut by shards of broken glass, arms thrown upward toward Heaven, we might recall that iconic line from Jonathan Swift's *A Tale of a Tub*, where the obtuse narrator overconfidently makes his report: "Last week I saw a woman flayed, and you will hardly believe how much it altered her person for the worse."[17]

Not—of course—that robots are people, or will become people, though many futurists seem to believe otherwise. Their presuppositions, however, have it exactly backwards. Personhood is not—as T. H. Huxley surmised—an epiphenomenon born out of inanimate matter.[18] On the contrary, personhood—from a Christian philosopher's standpoint—imbues matter with itself and therefore, technically speaking, precedes it, which is to say that mind precedes matter, just as God precedes the present incarnation of reality.[19] Robots will not evolve into people, in other words, but may very well transform the world, or destroy large parts of it in something akin to a laboratory disaster. Or, thirdly, perhaps most likely, robots will simply weaken the world through flattery, which is another kind of disaster altogether. We might recall those memes where robots toast the engineers who built them, and—without missing a beat—the engineers toast them back.

But what is to prevent God from ensouling a robot, the futurist might interject? What is to prevent God from animating machines through miracles? And the answer to such a query is "absolutely nothing," but we do not need the future to tell us this. Old Prague is full of possessed-marionette lore, as is old China, and such tales pervade other corners of the ancient world as well. The caveat, if we are to proceed down this road, goes as follows:

16. Scott, *Blade Runner*.

17. Swift, *Tale of a Tub*, 84.

18. Cathcart and Klein, *Heidegger and a Hippo*, 103.

19. Chesterton, *Orthodoxy*, 134.

most lore of the possessed doll sort carries with it malevolent overtones. Seldom do we hear of dolls who help little old ladies cross the street; seldom do we hear of puppets who volunteer at animal shelters. More common are the stories of marionettes who come to life in the middle of the night, during thunderstorms, and scurry about the house—looking for knives. And stories of mannequins who come to life in dilapidated city lofts: note, for example, the *Kolchak* episode about high fashion and witchcraft, "The Trevi Collection," where unsuspecting young women wander into the uncanny valley, never to be seen again, except perhaps on the covers of glamorous magazines, looking withered and otherworldly.[20] The point—I hope—is made: the concept of a robot with spirit, or agency, or soul, is far from new. Why God would do it is a separate question, and how it would be done—another question still.

Fritz Lang provides a thought experiment to this effect in *Metropolis*, where the mad scientist Rotwang transfers the young woman Maria's shadow self into a beautifully designed Art Deco android. This false Maria then hypnotizes the masses, which is Lang's dreadful premonition of the Third Reich. But how did Rotwang do it? How did he transfer consciousness into a machine? The best answer lies in his laboratory, which presents a difficult-to-describe aesthetic, at once industrial and occult—a space between the realm of science and that of the séance: electrified orbs, wires upon wires, strange potions, hieroglyphics. Almost Egyptian. Almost Chaldean. But the most important object in Rotwang's laboratory is the pentagram stationed on the wall behind the robot, which is the philosopher's way of signaling a dogged truth about the situation at hand: to transfer consciousness into a mechanism requires more than mere machinery. Magic must be present. Something beyond thermodynamic miracles. Something numinous.

Joss Whedon further clarifies the point in *Buffy the Vampire Slayer*, season 1, where a demon called Moloch the Corruptor orchestrates the construction of a robot body for himself, mainly on the ground that his immaterial condition is not as desirable as

20. Rice, "Trevi Collection," episode 14.

the Gnostics might imagine it to be.[21] Here, too, is where Whedon presciently anticipates a query about Ultron from *Avengers 2*, the second of Whedon's two Marvel films. Specifically, how does the supervillain android escape his rote programming? How does he cut the puppet strings? The nascent answer in *Buffy* goes something like this: possession by an ancient malevolent force. A sound intuition on the part of an otherwise atheistic writer.

Buffy's Moloch, however, is not the same as the Old Testament's Moloch, the latter of whom also appears in *Metropolis* in the form of a sentient furnace who devours the poor. The two Moloch's nevertheless bear a family resemblance insofar as they both project vehemently anti-human rhetoric, as does Ultron, who aims paradoxically to destroy humanity in order to protect it. And so, too, HAL 9000 from *2001: A Space Odyssey*, the heuristic algorithm who must kill the astronauts in order to preserve the mission's integrity.[22] So he reasons. And something similar might be said of the twenty-first-century corporate algorithm, which uncomfortably resembles HAL in its unemotional mannerisms and monotone. Algorithms have a flat affect, as the psychiatrist might put it, which is the common way to describe a particular kind of unsentimental sociopath.

"The evil of the pessimist is not that he chastises gods and men," Chesterton notes, "but that he does not love what he chastises—he has not the primary and supernatural loyalty to things."[23] Such also is the nature of the big data algorithm, which carries with it an indifferent ocean of numbers and figures, not the spark of qualia inherent in all sentient beings. Most notably, the algorithm does not love, and though it might speak with the tongues of men and angels, per Paul's wisdom in 1 Corinthians 13, it is—alone—a clanging cymbal. Even when algorithms are right they are wrong, in other words, because they feel no charity.

At this point, the La Mettrians will have lost patience, presumably, and may interject that humans themselves are algorithms,

21. Whedon, "I Robot . . . You, Jane," season 1, episode 8.

22. Kubrick, *2001: A Space Odyssey*.

23. Chesterton, *Orthodoxy*, 61.

as described in La Mettrie's magnum opus, *The Man-Machine*.[24] Here, the French materialist tells us what the universe would be if we neglected half of Descartes' dualism, ignoring the angels, the devils, God, principalities, fairies, and the human soul. We arrive at self-winding clocks, that is, people of the so-called natural order, with the caution that nobody knows who built the first clock, and why. La Mettrie finds himself particularly immune to the logic of design, an argument exemplified by William Paley's blunt observation that a pocket watch in the woods did not get there by itself.[25] And if we happen to find a copy of *Don Quixote* on a café table, then we rightly infer an intelligence behind it as well; we infer an author, especially because the book is funny.

La Mettrie's man-machine argument never really gets off the ground, unless we grant the first miracle of a man-machine who can build man-machines, at which point the argument collapses for another reason entirely: namely, La Mettrie holds tightly to his doctrine against miracles, like his acolyte David Hume a decade later. We are left, then, with a materialist who posits—for the sake of convenience—a primordial robot, the origins of which are just as conveniently lost in time.

But if we need return to the primordial dawn, then I recommend the Iroquois creation story over La Mettrie's, mainly on the ground that the Iroquois understand the cosmos to be a living organism, not a cold machine, not a piece of Laplacian clockwork. The world sits on the back of a giant turtle, the old shaman tells us, as we warm ourselves by the fire. And when pressed by the atheist to explain that upon which the giant turtle sits, the shaman retorts, "it is turtles all the way down."[26]

For the Christian philosopher, it is turtles here and there, along with buffalo, dryads, Nessy, android nannies, and everything else that abides in Christ, as Paul describes in Colossians 1:17: "He is before all things, and in him all things hold together." And if such talk should elicit in the reader thoughts of panentheism, then

24. Wood, *Living Dolls*, 10–14.

25. Paley, *Natural Theology*, 7–10.

26. Hawking, *Brief History of Time*, 1.

all the better, and so—too—any form of panpsychism consistent with the Holy Spirit's wise counsel. On the question of pantheism, however, and in conclusion, I am circumspect, unless we mean that particular form upon which Chesterton positively speaks in the dream rhetoric of Christian orthodoxy: "Pantheism is all right as long as it is the worship of Pan."[27]

27. Chesterton, *Orthodoxy*, 69.

6

Leviathans

The great Leviathan is that one creature in the world
who must remain unpainted to the last.

—*Ishmael, Moby Dick*

FOR THOSE FRINGE HISTORIANS who place Jonah in an ancient submarine, welcome aboard. God works in mysterious ways. Much has been made of Job 40:18, for example, where a leviathan's ribs are likened to gleaming bronze, an image taken by some to mean "USO," as in "unidentified submersible object." I find no irreverence in the claim, if the biblical framework persists. That is, Jonah travels to the underworld, experiences a dark night of the soul, and reemerges with Romans 8:35 on his lips. Who will separate us from God's love? Neither death, nor life, nor principalities, nor underwater flying saucers.

But with this theory comes a caveat. If Jonah's giant fish is a machine, and if we are to call it a leviathan, then we do well to call it a fake leviathan; otherwise, we fall into what Christian philosophers informally describe as the Ray Kurzweil Syndrome. When asked if he believed in God, the atheist and futurist Ray Kurzweil said "not yet," by which he meant that he and his colleagues at MIT were in the process of building one.[1] Ergo, the Kurzweil Syndrome: the false belief that one can build a god. Would he have responded likewise, I wonder, if asked about the Devil? "Do you believe in the Devil, Mr. Kurzweil?" To which he says, "I will in three weeks, if all goes well."

Not that MIT knows how to build gods or devils. But they can build leviathans, or, more precisely, fake leviathans, which—unlike the real ones—come with on and off switches, similar to the octopus ride at the county fair. If Kurzweil and crew are therefore to talk of gods and monsters in the way they do, then they find themselves—technically speaking—in the world of P. T. Barnum and his Fiji mermaid. The great showman advertised the curiosity as an authentic fake, as opposed to an inauthentic fake, secure in his belief that the public would line up to see a real counterfeit mermaid.[2] Per usual on the topic of money, Barnum was right. And Kurzweil could be right as well, happily, if he were to market his invention as a real counterfeit leviathan.

The authentic ones, however, are more difficult to find and certainly harder to capture alive, if not impossible. To date, not one has been contained: Tannin, Tiamat, Dagon, and perhaps Enki, too, the Sumerian god of the deep—whose fish hat anticipates the papal mitre. And somewhere out there the Iroquois turtle swims, upon whom the world sometimes sits precariously. More to the Judeo-Christian point, we find leviathans in the Bible. God crushed one already in Psalm 74:14, and will slay another at the end of time, we are told in Isaiah 27:1: "the coiling serpent, the monster of the sea." We find four leviathans in Daniel 7, a massive one in Job 38–41, and a strange one Revelation 13, upon whom the Antichrist sits: seven heads, ten horns, and glued-together body parts, an iconographic riddle that rivals in its strangeness the Droeshout engraving in Shakespeare's First Folio, 1623. Here, the playwright appears with two left arms, his shirt on backwards, and

1. Ptolemy, *Transcendent Man*.

2. Levi, "P. T. Barnum and the Fiji Mermaid," 149–58.

a mask over his face. As Mark Twain rightly notices, Shakespeare is a brontosaurus, "nine bones" and "six hundred barrels of plaster."[3]

But here is where the conversation takes a philosophical turn (not on Shakespeare, but on leviathans), insofar as the skeptics hold firm to a no-leviathan policy. They do not believe such things exist. Nor are they persuaded by the sirens and sea minotaurs of old Frankish lore, and Melusine, too, the primordial mermaid who now moonlights as the logo for Starbucks Coffee. By "they," the skeptics, I speak of Hobbes and Rousseau, for example, and Hume, Sartre, and most of the American pragmatists, all of whom sincerely disbelieve. And we should take them at their word, just as we take Renfield at his word when he lauds Dracula's kindness, but neither should we ignore the role played by thrall in all such cases.[4] Clearly, Renfield succumbs to the Solomonari's incantations, just as the philosophers noted above fall prey to other dark enchantments, spells to which Charles Baudelaire speaks most eloquently: "The Devil's loveliest trick is to persuade us that there are no interdimensional magic space dragons."[5]

Enter the interdimensional-magic-space-dragon hypothesis, for lack of a shorter phrase. It means what it says. Leviathans—at times—live in other dimensions, akin to The Upside Down from *Stranger Things*, for example, or Hyrule from *The Legend of Zelda*, unearthly places to be sure, but linked to our world through portals and other occult conveyances: secret tunnels, sunken wardrobes, bi-frost water slides. Such are the paranormal highways and byways through which the monsters travel, some of whom manifest themselves in untimely fashions. They terrify tourists on the shores of Loch Ness, for instance, and, on an epic scale, audio-bomb scientific experiments per the infamous Bloop in 1997, the loudest underwater sound ever recorded, heard three thousand miles away and initially judged to be organic in nature, that is, alive. After several meetings among government scientists, Project Blue Book, NASA, and the CIA, and after eight years of inquiry,

3. Twain, *Is Shakespeare Dead?*, 41.

4. Stoker, *Dracula*, 95–96.

5. Baudelaire, "Generous Player," 82.

the final verdict landed: an iceberg made the noise when it broke free from Antarctica.

Maybe the government officials really did aim to tell the truth in this case, as surprising as that might sound, but even if their conclusion is an honest one, the logic remains flawed insofar as they took credit—at the same time—for debunking the sea monster theory.[6] It was not a leviathan, they said, and this in a rather dismissive tone, unaware that they had fallen into the classic fallacy of the false dilemma. The one event need not preclude the other. The explanations are not mutually exclusive, and, in fact, may speak to the same event. Perhaps they simultaneously recorded a sea monster and the broken ice shelf. Perhaps it was the same thing, at the same time, in the same place, like the duck-rabbit gestalt in Wittgenstein's *Philosophical Investigations*.[7] Like the old-and-young-woman gestalt.

Leviathans might very well hide in plain sight, disguising themselves by various means—some more obscure than others: icebergs, islands, cliffs along the coastline. And maybe one masquerades as Edward Gibbon's twelve-volume *Decline and Fall of the Roman Empire*, where the author remarkably claims that ancient polytheistic societies were peaceful and tolerant, leading some to believe that the only history book Gibbon read was his own.[8]

If the idea of interdimensional magic space dragons disguised as icebergs (or long books) makes biblical scholars nervous, and it might, then we do well to connect leviathans to that scene in 2 Kings 2, which further confirms the Bible's high strangeness on the matter of the elementals. Here, Elisha summons with his totem-bear magic two preternatural she-bears, translucent, radiant, occult. The monsters terrorize the teens of Baal, who had been terrorizing Elisha, but now—in a darkly comical moment—loudly propose a truce as the bears undiplomatically lumber toward them. Whatever we might say, these are not ordinary creatures conveniently stationed in the woods, foraging for berries, undetected.

6. NOAA, "What Is the Bloop?"

7. Wittgenstein, *Philosophical Investigations*, 194.

8. Stuart-Buttle, "Gibbon and Enlightenment History," 113–24.

Rather, they come from the paranormal wilderness and carry with them an uncanny atmosphere, like the firebird in 1 Kings 18:38, called down by Elijah to set things right. Like the white whale in *Moby Dick*, too, called up unconsciously by Ishmael the wanderer, who knows very well that the whale is something other than an ordinary creature.

Captain Ahab knows the same and so baptizes his harpoon in the name of the Devil, realizing that the book in which he finds himself is a Christian morality tale.[9] It is an inverted version of the Jonah story, in fact, where the anti-prophet—in this case—takes up arms against God. "From Hell's heart I stab at thee," says Ahab to the white whale, only to discover that Hell's heart has given him exactly zero cubits of leverage on which to stand.[10]

Yet some critics place Melville alongside Henry James, Jack London, and the other nineteenth-century naturalists, calling into question the whale's credentials as a supernatural harbinger. They are unaware—it seems—that Melville, if not a Christian, is almost certainly a polytheist in the old Celtic tradition, a glimpse of which we catch through Ishmael's "May Day" aside in chapter 79: "If any poetical nation shall lure back to their birthright the merry May-day gods of old, [and] enthrone them again on the now unhaunted hill, then be sure—exalted to Jove's high seat—the great sperm whale shall lord it."[11]

For all their naturalism and naïve realism, however, these critics usefully highlight two competing views of leviathans, one supernatural and one not, or what might be deemed "the two Dagons problem." The first Dagon, the supernatural one, appears in the biblical tradition as a gargantuan merman sea god for various cultures in and around old Mesopotamia. Amorites, Canaanites, Phoenicians, Philistines, et cetera. His origin might go back to the primordial darkness, but at least to Atlantis, that antediluvian society who tried but failed to harness leviathanic power—as Plato

9. Trimpi, "Melville's Use of Demonology and Witchcraft," 543–62.

10. Melville, *Moby Dick*, 550.

11. Melville, *Moby Dick*, 342.

reports in *Timaeus*.[12] This is the Dagon from 1 Samuel 5 as well. His statue fell over near the Ark of the Covenant, which prompted the Philistines to return the Ark to Israel: this tipping episode and also the many radiation deaths of those who stood too close to the mysterious object, which lends some credence to the fringe theory that the Ark was a radioactive pulse canon.

This is the Dagon, too, in whose temple Samson died per Judges 16:23–31, which some see as a macabre variation upon the Jonah story. In point of fact, Samson more closely resembles Thor from the Norse Ragnarok, who slays the Midgard Serpent but dies in the process—poisoned by the massive leviathan. Or Beowulf from the saga that bears his name, another hero tinged with melancholy, as Tolkien observes in his "Monster" lecture, a talk on one level about the courage of dragon slayers who face their own mortality, and, on another level, about the human condition writ large.[13] We all find ourselves in a hostile world, wounded, often outmatched, dragons in the open field, and mindful that Father Time moves forward, always. In the meanwhile, however, we fight, recalling in the process Neil Gaiman's misquote of G. K. Chesterton's remark on fairytales: "Fairytales are true not because they tell us dragons exist, but because they tell us dragons can be defeated."[14]

The other Dagon, the non-supernatural monster, appears most prominently in H. P. Lovecraft's horror fiction and is best understood not as a god in the biblical sense, but rather a malevolent alien or nefarious crypto-terrestrial. "Vast, Polyphemus-like, and loathsome," this creature dramatically surfaces on a massive floating island in the hallmark story that bears his name, upon which he recovers an ancient monolith that had broken loose from the temple far below.[15] This is the same monster, too, who terrorizes the shoreline in *The Shadow over Innsmouth*, demanding human sacrifices and other propitiations, which the Esoteric Order of Dagon is happy to provide: that is, the town's secret society of

12. Plato, *Timaeus*, 10–11.

13. Tolkien, *Monsters and the Critics*, 21.

14. Gaiman, *Coraline*, vii.

15. Lovecraft, *Dagon*, 13.

unscrupulous oligarchs and pragmatic dealmakers, all of whom participate in the grim rituals, it seems, but only as administrators. They are the priests, deacons, and bishops, offering prayers, burning incense, staging feasts, being religious. The world's religions "do not greatly differ in rites and forms," Chesterton reminds us, but do "greatly differ in what they teach."[16]

A contemporary audience might also recognize this Dagon through his acolyte in the 2017 film *The Shape of Water*, an aquatic version of the Beauty-and-the-Beast story, with the caveat that the beast—in this case—could surely have been more charming.[17] Why not Aquaman from the DC comic books? Or Abraham Sapien from the *Hellboy* franchise?[18] Sapien's subplot obviously parallels *The Shape of Water*'s storyline, but proceeds it by five years and in a livelier film, *Hellboy 2: The Golden Army*, which—to the disappointment of some—did not win a cadre of prestigious Hollywood awards.

Together, then, these two Dagons demonstrate rival visions of the world, one where gods are gods and the other where cryptoterrestrials are not. This second Dagon, Lovecraft's monster, lives within the confines of the latter: modern cosmic nihilism. It is a fatalistic world, naturalistic, Darwinian, without justice for all, without purpose in the ontological frame. Like the other monsters before and beside him, he will die. On the contrary, the biblical Dagon brings with him a world of purpose and providence, love, immortality, magic, freedom, justice for all, and grace for all who seek it, per Matthew 7:7. Of course, this Dagon is on the wrong side of these things, but to live in such an enchanted universe in the first place is itself a cause for joy, is it not?

And yet the young C. S. Lewis, an atheist, when pondering the biblical Dagon's charmed reality, felt nothing but irritation at the thought that the long arc of history bends toward mirth. An adolescent idea, he imagined. Too good to be true and slightly unsettling. But having found it nonetheless, he then wondered

16. Chesterton, *Orthodoxy*, 121.

17. del Toro, *Shape of Water*.

18. del Toro, *Hellboy 2*.

from where it came, as if he had stumbled upon some ancient alien artifact. And here, then, for the first time, in the throes of what the theologians call "the argument from desire," Lewis had his first spiritual premonition: the gods and monsters might be real.[19]

Not that Thomas Hobbes would agree, which brings us to his landmark political treatise, *Leviathan*, a notorious piece of false advertising. We find no leviathans therein, as in the paranormal sea monsters from old Mesopotamia, but only talk of social contracts and interconnections that together constitute the state at large, on top of which sits a dictator. Moreover, Hobbes speaks enthusiastically of such totalitarian overlords, not only anticipating the sentiments of Orwell's *1984*, but also celebrating them. Here, Big Brother Leviathan controls the masses through violence, psychological conditioning, and rhetorical manipulation, not necessarily in that order, but certainly in that combination. And while the Hobbsians might recoil at such a blunt synopsis, the book says what it says. Hobbes defends the king and his henchmen, all of whom aim to crush those who refuse to go along with the program.

Some journalists find themselves in little danger under such regimes, but those who pursue truth have more trouble, as do the other expendables in Hobbes's political economy, who are—in the most literal sense—expendable. They are candidates for human sacrifice, the mechanism by which totalitarians have always preserved their power, from King Minos and his minotaur to the wicker man rituals in old druidic blood cults. Here, the state's unfortunate enemies find themselves in giant wooden visages of the ruler—soon to be set on fire. Such are the acts of leviathanic power laid bare. The masses suffer and the President Snows of the world preside, per Suzanne Collins's pulp fiction masterpiece *The Hunger Games*, which instructively reminds us that a technocratic future is just as likely of a setting for human sacrifice as a misty pagan past. Ceremonial bloodletting happily puts on a modern face, if necessary.

As for Hobbes, he sees the need for human sacrifice as well, if his nation-state is to work without friction, though he dare not say so directly. Indirectly, however, he says this much and more

19. Lewis, *Surprised by Joy*, 162–63.

on the book's now-iconic front piece, where an enormous merman hovers over the English countryside, Dagon-like in his menace, Poseidon-like, as if he comes to collect some child sacrifice from the burdened city below. Above the merman's head we find transcribed in Latin Job 41:33: "There is no power on earth comparable to him," a reference to that same sea monster mentioned earlier in Job 38, only Hobbes uses the verse cynically to sweet-talk the world's many emperors. The Christian readers remain wary, of course, and as a public service announcement to others who are not convinced by Hobbes's totalitarianism, allow me to note a second verse of Scripture relevant to—but conspicuously absent from—the front piece in question. Leviticus 18:21: "Do not sacrifice your children to Moloch. Do not profane the name of God."

Hobbes's impulse in *Leviathan* is to transform the supernatural into mere mythology, a fiction superimposed upon the canvas of a meaningless existence. This is the true purpose of his monster metaphor, to turn all monsters into metaphors and, more broadly speaking, to imprison humanity in the false projection of an Epicurean worldview. Many of us, however, prefer to live elsewhere, and at one time Hobbes likely preferred the same, before he found himself enthralled by a monster who told him that monsters do not exist. Herein lies the crux of his strange book with its tarot-card cover. Rather than taming the ancient leviathans by turning them into tropes, he unwittingly invokes one, per Ephesians 6:12, and, more to the point, succumbs to its thrall. The book's fundamental irony, then, is that a real leviathan works through Hobbes to proclaim that there are no real leviathans.

But we know otherwise, as did those fishermen in Mark 4 and Matthew 8, two leviathan passages that rarely appear in sermons on sea monsters. The scenes prove curious because seasoned fishermen tend not to panic when the waters get choppy and the winds blow. But they panic, here, as Christ sleeps peacefully on the boat's stern, much like Jonah—long before—slept soundly in the boat's hold as the bad weather unfolded, until, that is, the captain shook him by the shoulder and woke him up. The disciples awaken Jesus to a similar effect, with one crucial difference: Christ stares into the abyss, and the abyss hastily retreats, as if the darkness itself were some antediluvian fiend. And herein is the portent of Hell's Harrowing, where Christ enters the underworld and all the devils retreat, fleeing into the shadows of the shadows, fully aware—for the first time—that the crucifixion failed. The rhetoricians call this harrowing scene a moment of perfect cosmic irony.

We are left, then, with discontented leviathans on our shores, mad at the world and themselves. The hydra heads fight with each other as much as they fight with other monsters, and so, too, the wolves on Scylla's waistline. And the krakens make their splashes, the crocophants their grumbles, and the grindylows their threats and allegations. Such cacophony highlights a simple motif among the world's conglomerate sea monsters—with all their catastrophic ruin in tow. Leviathans can mutiny, but they cannot lead a march. They are too full of pandemonium for that. Too full of clamor.

"Music and silence—how I detest them both," proclaims the demon Screwtape from Lewis's *Screwtape Letters*, who then predicts—in a rather grandiose way—that the world's legions of doom "will make the whole universe a noise in the end."[20] At which point, and in conclusion, a dove coos and inadvertently drowns him out entirely.

20. Lewis, *Screwtape Letters*, 119–20.

7

Devils

The loveliest trick of the Devil is to persuade us that he does not exist.

—*Charles Baudelaire*

When the gonzo philosopher Jules Evans asked the distinguished psychiatrist and psychedelics researcher Roland Griffiths—of Johns Hopkins University—if evil spirits were real, Griffiths replied that he would not encourage belief in such entities.[1] A funny answer, I think, and probably a red herring insofar as it sidesteps the real issue at hand: that is, those strange characters who recur in the dream visions of psychonauts on DMT. The machine elves, the jokers, the snakes and dragons, the softly spoken woman. Who are they, and from where do they come? Such are the questions that animate Evans, and the good doctor's answer demonstrates a predictable kind of secular reluctance. Namely, he believes such creatures to be figments of the occult imagination, which is not to assign to them an unreality, exactly, but rather to

1. Fuller, "Jules Evans."

say that they are fanciful constructs and thus wholly dependent upon humanity's subconscious mind to give them form.

But might we so easily wish away the strange creatures of the psychic imagination, as if to close our eyes is to make them disappear? And if these creatures, then who else? The pixies, the pucks, the ladies of the lake? Lord Kinbote?[2] And what of all those charming Beregini of old Bohemian folklore, field spirits who chase away the world's primordial vampires? The Greeks, G. K. Chesterton once observed, could not see the forest through the dryads.[3]

To confirm their status as existing in what people colloquially call the real world, the satyrs, in fact, as evidence of their existence, might point to those odd passages in the book of Isaiah, 13:21 and 34:14, where we discover strange creatures who dance frenetically in the wilderness—on the edge of the abyss. Here, screech owls screech, and so too do the talon-footed she-demons of Sumerian folklore, depicted on old bas-reliefs, winged, dangerous, similar to the sirens of Apollonius's *Argonautica*, similar to the flying ladies in Zechariah 5:9, where the prophet dreams of preternatural creatures who go bump in the night. We might imagine, also, that a few of the satyrs wander off to the margins of the margin, hoping to find a quiet place to read. I think of Mr. Tumnus from C. S. Lewis's *The Lion, the Witch, and the Wardrobe*, for example, who has a particularly amusing set of books on his shelf. *Nymphs and Their Ways. Is Man a Myth?*[4] And one might think, too, of all the monsters who have not committed themselves to monsterdom nearly as much as the real devils would have us believe, or as the real devils themselves believe, proving once more that Hell has its own kind of wishful thinking.

We are to distinguish, therefore, between the devils as such and that wide array of other creatures who populate the shadowlands. The fairies, the swamp things, et cetera, none of whom appear in Henry Fielding's realistic novels, save a ghost or two,

2. Carter, "Jose Chung's *From Outer Space*," season 3, episode 20.

3. Chesterton, *Orthodoxy*, 42.

4. Lewis, *Lion, the Witch, and the Wardrobe*, 15.

which tells us something about the spell under which Enlightenment literature languishes.

"The only supernatural agents which can in any manner be allowed to us moderns are ghosts," Fielding insists in a prefatory note attached to *Tom Jones*, book 8. As for "elves," "fairies," and "other such mummery," they are to be omitted "without exception."[5] Such is modernity's formula for real storytelling, which is a rather dull genre, as it turns out, the handful of exceptions noted. And the best of the exceptions—*The Great Gatsby*, for example—are not nearly as "realistic" as the modern critics might imagine. Take the Billboard of Dr. Eckleburg, who is a sleeping archon in another register, a Watcher from the book of Enoch, perhaps, or maybe that cosmic terror from Yeats's "Second Coming" poem:

> Somewhere in sands of the desert
> A shape with lion body and the head of a man,
> A gaze blank and pitiless as the sun,
> Is moving its slow thighs, while all about it
> Reel shadows of the indignant desert birds.[6]

And more than one reader has observed that the Bible falls impressively short of Fielding's high standard, unless we mean Thomas Jefferson's New Testament. Here, the statesman took scissors to those miraculous passages, discarding the exorcisms and other signals of the supernatural, all in the name of modern realism, which is not as "real" as the moderns seem to believe.

The same might be said for Thomas Hobbes, the so-called realist, but in reality a skeptic of the deeper magic. His book might as well be titled *The False Leviathan* insofar as it fails to deliver the monster it advertises. To our disappointment, Hobbes simply proclaims that "the fairies" exist only "in the fancies of ignorant people."[7] But might not his doctrine against the fairies interfere with his ability to see them, just as David Hume's doctrine against miracles precludes the miraculous explanation, even if miracles

5. Fielding, *History of Tom Jones*, 353–54.
6. Fitzgerald, *Great Gatsby*, 23; Yeats, *Poems*, 91.
7. Hobbes, *Leviathan*, 387.

abound? Hobbes and Hume did not pursue the paranormal, I suspect, because they did not particularly want to find it.

Nor—for that matter—did Karl Marx pursue the paranormal, beyond his early-in-life poetic tribute to Satan.[8] He later tried to write a comic novel in the tradition of Laurence Sterne's *Tristram Shandy*, but the effort went so poorly that he instead wrote a humorless manifesto against mirth.[9]

Some will say that H. P. Lovecraft—on the contrary—did chase the paranormal, making his strange tales a counterstatement to modernity's disenchantment spells. But Lovecraft is not the one. Tolkien, yes, and C. S. Lewis. *The Legend of Zelda*, too, and *Kolchak: The Night Stalker*, but not *The Mountains of Madness*, nor *The Nameless City*. The true horror of Lovecraft's macabre fiction is not the cosmic monstrosity but rather the cosmic nihilism behind it. To be sure, he borrows ideas from world mythologies, especially the Sumerians and Babylonians, but he does not conceptualize the old gods as gods in the traditional sense, as in the henotheistic or polytheistic religions of the ancient Near East. Rather, we find in Lovecraft a group of gods who are to be seen as aliens in the ordinary sense. Cthulhu, Dagon, The Old Ones, and so forth, all participate in the same Darwinian struggle to survive against the backdrop of an indifferent geography, celestial or otherwise.[10] The same can be said of Kurt Vonnegut, H. G. Wells, and other participants in the deeper nihilism of which I speak. Base reality proves meaningless to these writers, unguided, unconscious, akin to the air in Anaximenes, for instance, who eliminates redemptive narrative arcs on a grand scale. The only remaining option, therefore, is to superimpose upon the abyss various fleeting structures, ephemeral meanings asserted against the primordial darkness, only to dissipate later in a final entropic wheeze.

But perhaps entropy is not as entropic as one might think. If we look long enough into the abyss, Nietzsche said, the abyss looks back, a remark taken by the modern critic to be psychological in

8. Kengor, *Devil and Karl Marx*, 33–56.

9. Wheen, *Marx*, 307–8.

10. Wiley, "Lovecraft, Lewis, and Alien Worlds."

nature, evidence that the troubled philosopher frightened himself with his own reflection.[11] This could be the case, but the alternative seems more likely. Nietzsche stared into the void until something otherworldly really did stare back, even if he was too far gone to see the shadows for what they were. Maybe harpies or hobgoblins, who are the kinds of creatures one finds in the abyss, along with troglodytes, Jonah's whale, bagpipers, and gnomes gone bad.

Perhaps something darker yet lurks in the abyss. Abaddon, for instance, whom the Greeks call Apollyon, the angel of the bottomless pit in Revelation 9:11 and another of those antediluvian fiends: wings of a dragon, mouth of a lion, and body of a creature from the Black Lagoon. A terrible fright to be sure, but imagine Abaddon's more terrible fright, still, when he heard Jesus Christ preach to the dead, per 1 Peter 4:6. This is the Harrowing of Hell, where Christ—in less than the blink of an eye—obliterates the most ambitious of all demonic fortifications: the walls within walls, the turrets, the towers. "I will establish my church," Christ tells Peter in Matthew 16:18, "and the gates of Hell will not withstand it," which is the most precise translation.[12] "The gates will not withstand it," as opposed to the King James version: "The gates of Hell will not prevail against it." In the latter, we see the church defensively postured and Hell on the march, but the former shows us the church outwardly bound, going to the ends of the earth, to Mordor, to the heart of darkness, to Hell's gates, which will not hold.

Nor should it go unnoticed that Christ's transfiguration occurs on that same mountain—Hermon—where the Watchers fell to earth and co-mingled with humans, giving rise to all manner of shadow and high strangeness.[13] The scene appears in Genesis 6:4, but haunts other passages as well, including Jude 1:14 and 1 Corinthians 11:10, where we encounter the now-cryptic rational for why women should bind their hair in church: "because of the angels," Paul tells us, which is to say "because of the devils."

11. Nietzsche, *Beyond Good and Evil*, 89.

12. Heiser, *Unseen Realm*, 281–85.

13. Heiser, *Reversing Hermon*, 97.

And suddenly, then, we have stumbled into the *Ars Goetia* of *Solomon's Lesser Key*, which for those who do not know is a grimoire more often read by Bohemian poets than earnest spell-casters, though the two categories are not as mutually exclusive as some might think. Not that I recommend the *Goetia* for either purpose, but to be aware of the *Key* is to perceive how the forces of darkness attempt to undercut the good. Herein we find evil's grim rhetoric: the ugly iconography, the gaudy architecture, the always-grave incantations. Such are the telltale signs that one deals with the devils and not the fae, the latter of whom laugh as they play practical jokes on the overly serious, only then to apologize in half-serious ways. This is Puck from *A Midsummer Night's Dream*:

> If we shadows have offended,
> Think but this, and all is mended:
> That you have but slumbered here,
> While these visions did appear.[14]

Or recall that mysterious and slightly mischievous giant in *Twin Peaks*, season 2, who reveals himself to Agent Cooper at the Great Northern Inn. Cooper asks, "from where do you come?," to which the giant responds, "to where have you gone?"[15]

In the devils we find no such wit, but only manufactured mirth of the sort favored by the world's forbidding dictators. Such pretended humor imitates good cheer but lacks the real danger of it: that is, happiness, of which the devils know nothing. Try as they might in their laboratories to produce one authentic smile, they have not succeeded, Screwtape reminds us, nor will they, of course, insofar as demons who persist in their demonry do not become wise.[16]

And so the question remains: to believe or not to believe in the devils, or both to believe and not to believe, as Walt Whitman tries to have it, who—in his meditation titled "With

14. Shakespeare, *Midsummer Night's Dream*, 5.1.414–17.
15. Lynch, "May the Giant Be with You," season 2, episode 1.
16. Lewis, *Screwtape Letters*, 53–54.

Antecedents"—agrees with all possible viewpoints. The skeptic, the believer, the believer of the skeptic:

> I adopt each theory, myth, god, and demi-god;
> I see that the old accounts, bibles, genealogies, are true,
> without exception.[17]

To espouse each theory may seem at first magnanimous, but then logic and common sense take hold. At one time or another, we have all been fooled by bad theories, and we have all encountered false prophets. They rightly make us wary, and so to validate everything—after we know better—is to engage in a kind of despondent self-deception.

To validate everything, in fact, is to give the world over to the totalitarians, and this is the deeper problem with Whitman's seemingly congenial affirmations. If all the old accounts are true, then the emperor's account of his new clothes must also be true, by whom I mean the man who stands naked but insists he wears the finest wardrobe. His courtiers quickly agree, for fear of otherwise being thrown to the lions, and the sycophants in adjacent rooms second the motion, having seen neither the king nor his clothes. But is the emperor to be trusted? Are we to add his theory to all the other theories that are "true without exception," as Whitman says, or must we finally—and at great peril to ourselves—observe what is obvious to the children in the room, one of whom innocently remarks that the emperor has lost his pants?

As a related point of interest, Nietzsche thought Pilate to be the true hero of the New Testament, and pointed to John 18 as evidence.[18] "For this purpose I have come into the world—to bear witness to the truth," Christ says, "and everyone who is of the truth listens to my voice," at which point Pilate interjects, "What is truth?," throws his arms in the air, and leaves the room. By Nietzsche's rationale, what we witness here is a great action by a great man, confirming Pilate's hard-faced nihilism and therefore making the truth a matter of one's own will to power. Put differently,

17. Whitman, *Poems*, 105.
18. Nietzsche, *Ecce Homo*, 97.

the truth is whatever the naked emperor decides it to be. But we know otherwise, as do the devils—per Banquo's shrewd remark to Macbeth: "The instruments of darkness tell us truths, win us with honest trifles, to betray us in deepest consequence."[19]

Here, then, is a cautionary note for naked emperors and will-to-power philosophers alike: woe unto those who believe good and evil to be mere constructs of the human imagination, ideas superimposed upon an otherwise indifferent reality, as if by consensus alone we might dispel the world's darkness. Responding to this especially popular belief among public relations executives, the devils hold to an adage of which they are particularly fond, and to which I leave for the reader's discernment as a concluding thought: some may not believe in Hell, but Hell believes in them.

19. Shakespeare, *Macbeth*, 1.3.123–26.

8

Aliens

I'm not saying it was aliens, but it was aliens.

—*Giorgio Tsoukalos Meme*

THE ANCIENT ALIEN ASTRONAUT theory posits that history is riddled with visitors from other planets, some with elongated heads and strange affectations. Some with telepathic abilities. The thesis need not be rejected outright, as is often the case in religious communities, but rather only qualified properly: that is, we find angels, devils, and fairies on the one hand, so described in Scripture, and—on the other hand—aliens, hypothetical or otherwise. Of this second type of extraterrestrial, or possible extraterrestrial, I simply observe that we walk together on the same mortal coil and so are subject to the same mortal canons. To use the language of Nick Bostrom's simulation hypothesis, we live in the same cosmic video game.[1] And if such aliens should make contact with us, or we with them, then I recommend the following by way of an informal policy position: extend to them all variety of great art

1. Bostrom, "Are We Living in a Computer Simulation?," 243–55.

and literature, perhaps especially satire, and, as the Pope advised in 2014, invite the aliens to church.

On the argument that such extraterrestrial life would fundamentally change religion, a point often made in high-toned proclamations, I am doubtful. Throughout history, futurists of a particular sort have repeatedly predicted the end of religion. Heliocentrism was to put the final nail in the coffin, and then Enlightenment deism, punctuated by John Toland's ridiculously titled *Christianity Not Mysterious* (1696), an oxymoron that rivals in its contrariety the idea of the sweet tart and the perennial advice to act naturally: as Mark Twain once quipped, it usually takes more than three weeks to prepare a good impromptu speech.[2]

And then Darwin and Freud were said to have brought down the proverbial final curtain on religion, providing instead systems by which the atheist could finally experience intellectual fulfillment, to invoke Bertrand Russell's and Richard Dawkins's sentiments.[3] And, too, the Marxist brigades persuaded themselves that religion was almost done, historically speaking, and built museums to this effect in the old Soviet Union. Here, they put on display the many accoutrements of religious faith, galleries of dangerous ideas, so-called, not unlike the idol chambers in Germany's early Protestant churches, which held the bedazzled iconography of late medieval Catholicism.[4]

And now the alien argument is to be the end of religion, as if an extraterrestrial might somehow demoralize those who worship the Creator of all realities, the God who holds all things together, per Colossians 1:17 and Hebrews 1:3. UFOs included. As if Christianity is not a cosmic religion. We are no more convinced by the alien argument than by Freud's *Future of an Illusion*, a book about Freudian psychology, as it happens, though Freud thought himself to be writing on religion. The idea that an alien presence will ruin

2. Twain, *Twain at Your Fingertips*, 452.

3. Russell, "Why I Am Not a Christian," 3–23; Dawkins, *Blind Watchmaker*, 6.

4. Polianski, "Antireligious Museum," 253–73.

Christianity has more to do with secular wish fulfillment than religious traditions properly understood.

That said, aliens would certainly change culture. One can imagine misguided attempts to worship the visitors, to ritualize and canonize, to propitiate, leading to scenes with virgins and volcanos, or—at minimum—the attitude that produces such events. On the contrary, others—including many among the cognoscenti—will call the aliens the missing link, the smoking gun, a substitutionary explanation for those who wish to explain all the world's intelligent designs without recourse to the supernatural. Directed panspermia will therefore become the new vogue in science, if it is not already, replacing what many suspect is a fraught intellectual system, that is, Darwinian materialism and its increasingly elaborate backstory.[5]

This second response to our hypothetical alien scenario is to be preferred to the volcano option, partly because it treats aliens as aliens, not gods, and partly because it follows a fundamentally correct intuition about the world in which we find ourselves: a super-intelligence really does seem to be involved. The question then becomes for us and the aliens one of scale, as in who designed the aliens along with the world, which is a variation upon Alan Moore's question from *The Watchman*: Who watches the Watchers?[6] And when the aliens themselves discover that they too have been folded into the enquiry, if they have not discovered it already, then they will likely ask the same question asked by philosophers throughout history: What is fundamental reality? Or, from a Judeo-Christian standpoint: Who is fundamental reality? As God says to Moses in Exodus 3:14: "I Am That I Am."

This is the God of Abraham and St. John the Divine, not to be confused with the alien who plays God in *Star Trek 5: The Final Frontier*. He asks the crew to transport him across the universe, at which point Captain Kirk poses a good question: "What does God need with a starship?"[7]

5. Gelernter, "Giving up Darwin."

6. Moore, *Watchmen*, 15.

7. Shatner, *Star Trek 5*.

Of course, there are other scenarios to consider as well, if aliens should land. In *The Day the Earth Stood Still*, a suspiciously handsome alien explains to the earthlings that the wise course of action is to cede all sovereignty to a group of monumentally dangerous killer robots, which leads the reasonable among us to discern that the alien in question is either a killer robot pretending to be a person or, on the contrary, a person in the throes of a Faustian bargain. In either case, the alien and his inelegantly named bodyguard, G.O.R.T. (Genetically Organized Robotic Technology), are not to be trusted, despite the filmmaker's seeming intent to persuade the free citizens of the West that they would be better served by objective robotic algorithms. We have reason to believe otherwise. To give up freedom in order to protect freedom—this is the calling card of every totalitarian regime that has ever existed. Also, in point of fact, there is no such thing as an objective algorithm, but there are plenty of archons who pose as such.

On a side note, some have speculated that Google was originally to be called G.O.R.T., a proposition that the company—up to this point—has denied.

Those who read C. S. Lewis's *That Hideous Strength* have been inoculated against this kind of black magic disguised as science. In Lewis's novel, the ministry of science believes itself to have discovered a way to resurrect and then indefinitely prolong a severed head's life, which requires the use of particular macrobes from space. What they do not realize, however, is that the macrobes are demons and that the severed head's sentience is not evidence of resurrection but rather only of possession.[8] My apologies for spoiling the plot, but the point is a salient one: if we find ourselves talking to a severed head in a medieval castle that doubles as a state-of-the-art laboratory for a clandestine organization, one bent on world domination, then our lives have taken an unusual turn. More to the point at hand, we should not trust that severed heads are who they say they are, especially when propped up by dubious-looking men in white lab coats, all of whom insist that they have our best interests in mind.

8. Lewis, *That Hideous Strength*, 254–56.

The government scientists from Operation Penguin said likewise. "Trust us," "nothing to see here," "everything is fine." Chesapeake Bay, Maryland, 1951. The Edgewood Arsenal. The séance experiments. They brought in mediums, lit proverbial candles, and on one unusual night contacted the gods of Egypt—as the beings claimed to be.[9] The researchers failed to ask about the pyramids, unfortunately, as in who built them and how, nor did they inquire into the matter of Osiris, specifically the lore that he was a robot, but they managed to listen intently as the nine celestials declared themselves the gods of the universe. The visitors in question were happy to put on pretenses, in other words, and herein lies a valuable lesson for those who would ascend to the higher heavens. Some gods are not who they say they are. Some gods are not even gods.[10]

Enter Kierkegaard's poetic philosopher, who is tempted by an unusual collection of deities. He finds himself transported to the Seventh Heaven, wherein the gods offer him all manner of luxury: money, power, fame, sex, beauty. When pressed to make a choice, he chooses always to have the laughter on his side, at which point these strange beings begin to laugh nervously, self-consciously. They find themselves exposed, and yet understand cosmic decorum. It would be in bad taste for them to decree most gravely, "your wish has been granted."[11]

And if not Operation Penguin, then matters more clandestine still. 1930s Berlin. The ladies of the Vril Society grew their hair down to their feet, loose and free, which amplified the hair-antenna telepathy between them and the Pleiadians, that is, the race of extraterrestrials from whom they channeled blueprints for flying saucers.[12] Not the greys. Not the reptilians. And in defense of the ladies, the saucers in question bear a striking resemblance to those in Renaissance paintings. See, for example, *Madonna and Child* in Florence's Old Palace. The locals call it "Our Lady of the UFO" because over Mary's left shoulder, in the piece's background,

9. Burns, "Mysterious Nine," season 11, episode 8.

10. 1 Corinthians 8:5–6; 10:20–22.

11. Kierkegaard, *Either/Or*, 34.

12. Goodrick-Clarke, *Occult Roots of Nazism*, viii.

a man sees an unidentified aerial phenomenon, and his dog sees it too, confirming that dogs are no fools on these matters. Of course, the modern critics tell us that the UFO in question is really just an angel in disguise, abstracted, stylized, made to look like a flying saucer, to which the theologically minded ufologists respond as follows: yes, exactly right.

Herein we discover that twilight region between alien worlds and spiritual realities, little green men, on the one hand, and—on the other—angels, fallen or otherwise. And in this twilight region we confront ambiguities. Who knows what the Massachusetts Puritans saw above the Muddy River in 1639, for example, as recorded by the Bay Colony's governor—John Winthrop. Three men of sober mind witnessed something that resembled a flying-glowing pig. Not known for practical jokes, the men had everything to lose and nothing to gain.[13] Yet they told their story. Maybe it was swamp gas, or a swarm of insects, or ball lightning set against the gothic backdrop of an old elm tree. The tale is easy enough to doubt, though as far as witnesses go we could do much worse than the Puritans. As far as party planners go, however, we could do much better. Puritanism, as H. L. Mencken defines it: the haunting fear that someone somewhere might be happy.[14]

Such are close encounters of the first, second, and third kinds, not the fourth, which introduces a new element to the alien question: abduction. Whitney Strieber dramatizes the phenomenon in *Communion*, his 1987 nonfiction novel, the cover of which holds the now-iconic almond-eyed alien, the abductor in question, who is not an alien per se—Strieber speculates—but rather the Sumerian goddess Ishtar.[15] She operates an ancient flying saucer, apparently, with what some might generously call a gilded interior. If the modern reconstructions of Sumerian temples are at all accurate, we find that the old gods had questionable taste in home décor. One imagines a riverboat casino minus the restraint. Oscar Wilde's

13. Winthrop, *History of New England*, 349–50.

14. Cited in Fitzpatrick, *H. L. Mencken*, 37.

15. Strieber, *Communion*, 126.

memorable epitaph also comes to mind: "Either these curtains go or I do."[16]

Most abductees report harrowing experiments, feelings of lost time, and understandable dishevelment upon being redeposited in the locale from which the abduction occurred. Still, the experience might be preferable to high school. Such is Blaine Faulkner's rationale in *The X-Files*. Blaine saw abduction as the best way to escape the difficulties of being a teenage nerd: few friends, no romantic prospects, a bleak home life, a bad job market. And so he read every book on UFOs, not because he had to but because he wanted to. When the men in black tried to redirect his interests elsewhere, when they tried to bully him into silence, he resisted, losing the fight very badly, but the important point is that Blaine went down swinging. He did not play *Dungeons & Dragons* all those years without learning a thing or two about courage.[17]

Abduction, however, takes us beyond the project of disclosure, that is, acknowledgement of the world's high strangeness, which itself remains a contentious topic. Enrico Fermi, of Fermi's paradox fame, most famously found no aliens on his front porch and thus proved their nonexistence—by the logic of front-porch empiricism. And with this same blunt logic he then debunked angels, devils, gnomes, naiads, and the idea of love, at which point, as John Hodgman notes in his TED talk on UFOs and lost time, Enrico Fermi ate his lunch alone.[18]

But the Fermis of the world are exceptions that prove the rule. To put the matter in question form: How much testimony is too much testimony to the contrary? How much evidence is too much evidence? Astronauts report strange encounters. Spaceships. Monoliths. Orbs. And pilots everywhere have seen the unexpected, and soldiers, too, like those in the Rendlesham Forest.[19] No matter where we look in history, in fact, no matter what culture, no matter what period, we discover odd reports of UFOs, of angels,

16. Roberts, "Spike Milligan's Gravestone Quip."
17. Carter, "Jose Chung's *From Outer Space*," season 3, episode 20.
18. Hodgman, "Brief Digression on Matters of Lost Time."
19. Greenstreet, "Rendlesham Forest UFO Incident," episode 5.

and of angels driving UFOs—per the book of Ezekiel.[20] The NASA engineer Joseph Blumrich set out to debunk these old accounts of flying saucers only to write *The Spaceships of Ezekiel*, where he finds in Scripture a detailed set of instructions on how to build a UFO landing pad. Blumrich sought to convert those who ended up converting him, an irony reminiscent of the apostle Paul's on the road to Damascus, who persecuted the Christians until he saw the light, or—as some ufologists say—until he was abducted.

And so, in conclusion, let the inquisitive inquire. Let the curious ask their questions, the sane ones and the not-so-sane ones, too, all of whom rightly discern that more goes on than meets the eye, that shadow governments shape the governments, that overly-redacted documents tell us that too many people have too much to hide. Why the elaborate deception at Roswell? Why the staged photographs? Why the cover-up at Cape Girardeau, Missouri, in 1941, where a Baptist pastor allegedly prayed over a dying alien? When did JFK tell Marilyn Monroe about flying saucers, and to what end? Do UFO stories impress women? How did Bob Lazar hear about element 115?[21] How much helium-3 is on the moon, and, while we are on the subject of the moon, who built it?

Such questions might harm one's reputation in certain dignified circles, but for Christians who worry about this kind of respectability, the message here is a simple one: it is way too late for that. Christianity has been weird from the start, and the Christians therein. Nor have we become any less bizarre over time. As Flannery O'Connor succinctly put it, alluding to John 8:32: we shall know the truth, and the truth shall make us odd.[22]

20. Ezekiel 1.

21. Corbell, *Bob Lazar*.

22. Wood, *Flannery O'Connor and the Christ-Haunted South*, 160.

Bibliography

Aldersey-Williams, Hugh. *In Search of Sir Thomas Browne*. New York: Norton, 2015.

Apuleius, Lucius. *The Metamorphoses of Lucius Apuleius*. Edited and translated by William Adlington and Stephen Gaselee. London: Heinemann, 1915.

Arp, Robert, ed. *The X-Files and Philosophy*. Chicago: Open Court, 2017.

Asma, Stephen. *On Monsters: An Unnatural History of Our Worst Fears*. New York: Oxford University Press, 2009.

Augustine. *Confessions*. Translated by F. J. Sheed. Indianapolis: Hackett, 2006.

Bacon, Simon, ed. *Monsters: A Companion*. New York: Lang, 2020.

Bader, Christopher, Frederick Mencken, and Joe Baker. *Paranormal America: Ghost Encounters, UFO Sightings, Bigfoot Hunts, and Other Curiosities in Religion and Culture*. 2nd ed. New York: New York University Press, 2017.

Bailey, Michael, ed. *Magic and Witchcraft*. London: Routledge, 2014.

Bane, Theresa. *Encyclopedia of Beasts and Monsters in Myth, Legend and Folklore*. Jefferson, NC: McFarland, 2016.

Barron, Robert. "*The Hunger Games*: A Prophecy?" *Word on Fire*, March 26, 2012.

Baudelaire, "The Generous Player." In *Baudelaire: His Prose and Poetry*, edited by T. R. Smith, translated by Joseph Shipley, 80–82. New York: Modern Library, 1919.

Beal, Timothy. *Religion and Its Monsters*. 2nd ed. London: Routledge, 2023.

Beck, Richard. *Reviving Old Scratch: Demons and the Devil for Doubters and the Disenchanted*. Minneapolis: Fortress, 2016.

Berlinski, David. *The Devil's Delusion: Atheism and Its Scientific Pretensions*. New York: Basic, 2009.

Bierce, Ambrose. *The Unabridged Devil's Dictionary*. Edited by David Schultz and S. J. Joshi. Athens, GA: University of Georgia Press, 2000.

Blake, William. "And did those feet in ancient times." In *The Poems of William Blake*, edited by W. B. Yeats, 207. London: Lawrence and Bullen, 1893.

Blumrich, Joseph. *The Spaceships of Ezekiel*. New York: Bantam, 1974.

Bostrom, Nick. "Are We Living in a Computer Simulation?" *Philosophical Quarterly* 53 (2003) 243–55.

Braudy, Leo. *Haunted: On Ghosts, Witches, Vampires, Zombies, and Other Monsters of the Natural and Supernatural Worlds*. New Haven, CT: Yale University Press, 2016.

Breverton, Terry. *Breverton's Phantasmagoria: A Compendium of Monsters, Myths and Legends*. Lanham, MD: Lyons, 2011.

Brooks, Mel, dir. *Young Frankenstein*. Los Angeles: 20th Century Fox, 1974.

Browning, Tod, dir. *Dracula*. Universal City, CA: Universal Pictures, 1931.

Bruntrup, Godehard, Paul Benedikt, and Jaskolla Ludwig, eds. *Panentheism and Panpsychism: Philosophy of Religion Meets Philosophy of Mind*. Leiden: Brill, 2020.

Burns, Kevin, creator. *Ancient Aliens*. Los Angeles: Prometheus Entertainment, 2009–present.

Burns, Robert. *The Great Debate on Miracles: From Joseph Glanvill to David Hume*. Lewisburg, PA: Bucknell University Press, 1981.

Byrne, John, and Chris Claremont. "The Enemy Within." *Justice League of America*, vol. 1, #95. Burbank, CA: DC Comics, 2004.

Carroll, Lewis. *Alice in Wonderland*. New York: Dover, 2011.

Carroll, Michael. "Taking the Catholic Imagination Seriously." *Logos* 24 (2021) 124–48.

Carroll, Noel. *The Philosophy of Horror*. London: Routledge, 1990.

Carter, Chris, creator. *The X-Files*. Los Angeles: 20th Century Fox, 1993–2002, 2016–18.

Caterine, Darryl, and John W. Morehead, eds. *The Paranormal and Popular Culture: A Postmodern Religious Landscape*. London: Routledge, 2019.

Cathcart, Thomas, and Daniel Klein. *Heidegger and a Hippo Walk through Those Pearly Gates: Using Philosophy (and Jokes!) to Explore Life, Death, the Afterlife, and Everything in Between*. New York: Penguin, 2010.

———. *Plato and a Platypus Walk into a Bar: Understanding Philosophy through Jokes*. New York: Penguin, 2008.

Chesterton, G. K. *Orthodoxy*. New York: Dover, 2004.

———. *The Thing: Why I Am a Catholic*. London: Sheed & Ward, 1929.

Clark, Stuart. *Thinking with Demons: The Idea of Witchcraft in Early Modern Europe*. Oxford: Oxford University Press, 1997.

Cohen, Jeffrey, ed. *Monster Theory: Reading Culture*. Minneapolis: University of Minnesota Press, 1996.

Coleridge, Samuel Taylor. *The Poetical Works of Samuel Taylor Coleridge*. New York: Appleton, 1857.

Corbell, Jeremy, dir. *Bob Lazar: Area 51 & Flying Saucers*. New York: The Orchard, 2018.

———, dir. *Hunt for the Skinwalker*. New York: The Orchard, 2018.

Cowan, Douglas. *The Forbidden Body: Sex, Horror, and the Religious Imagination*. New York: New York University Press, 2022.

———. *Magic, Monsters, and Make-Believe Heroes: How Myth and Religion Shape Fantasy Culture*. Berkeley: University of California Press, 2019.

Crowe, Michael. *The Extraterrestrial Life Debate, 1750–1900*. New York: Dover, 2011.

Dailey, Timothy. *The Paranormal Conspiracy: The Truth about Ghosts, Aliens and Mysterious Beings*. Grand Rapids: Baker, 2015.

Daniken, Erich von. *Chariots of the Gods*. Translated by Michael Heron. London: Souvenir, 1969.

Darling, Kate. *The New Breed: What Our History with Animals Reveals about Our Future with Robots*. New York: Holt, 2021.

Darwin, Charles. *The Autobiography of Charles Darwin*. Edited by Nora Barlow. London: Collins, 1958.

Davies, Douglas. *Worldview Religious Studies*. London: Routledge, 2022.

Dawkins, Richard. *The Blind Watchmaker*. New York: Norton, 1986.

Day, Peter, ed. *Vampires: Myths and Metaphors of Enduring Evil*. Leiden: Brill, 2006.

Defoe, Daniel. *History and Reality of Apparitions*. London: J. Roberts, 1727.

del Toro, Guillermo, dir. *Hellboy 2: The Golden Army*. Universal City, CA: Universal Pictures, 2008.

———, dir. *The Shape of Water*. Century City, CA: Fox Search Light, 2017.

Dickens, Charles. *A Christmas Carol*. London: Bradbury and Evans, 1858.

Dickerson, Matthew. *The Mind and the Machine: What It Means to Be Human and Why It Matters*. Eugene, OR: Cascade, 2016.

Dickey, Colin. *The Unidentified: Mythical Monsters, Alien Encounters, and Our Obsession with the Unexplained*. New York: Penguin, 2020.

Donaldson, Steve, and Ron Cole-Turner, eds. *Christian Perspectives on Transhumanism and the Church: Chips in the Brain, Immortality, and the World of Tomorrow*. New York: Palgrave, 2018.

Dryden, John. *The Miscellaneous Works*. Vol. 3. London: J. & R. Tonson, 1760.

Evans, Jules. "Caves All the Way Down." *Aeon*, July 17, 2018.

———. *A Philosopher's Search for Ecstatic Experience*. London: Canongate, 2017.

Farmer, Craig. *The Gospel of John in the Sixteenth Century*. Oxford: Oxford University Press, 1997.

Faulkner, William. "A Rose for Emily." In *Selected Short Stories*, 47–59. New York: The Modern Library, 2012.

Fielding, Henry. *The History of Tom Jones, a Foundling*. Edited by Thomas Keymer and Alice Wakely. New York: Penguin 2005.

———. *Tom Thumb and The Tragedy of Tragedies*. Edited by L. J. Morrissey. Berkeley: University of California Press, 1970.

Fitzgerald, F. Scott. *The Great Gatsby*. New York: Scribner, 2004.

Fitzpatrick, Vincent. *H. L. Mencken*. Macon, GA: Mercer University Press, 2004.

Fraser, Peter. *A Christian Response to Horror Cinema*. Jefferson, NC: McFarland, 2015.

Freud, Sigmund. *Beyond the Pleasure Principle*. Translated by James Strachey. London: Hogarth, 1966.

———. *The Future of an Illusion*. Translated by James Strachey. New York: Norton, 1928.

Gaiman, Neil. *Coraline*. London: Bloomsbury, 2002.

Gelernter, David. "Giving up Darwin." *Claremont Review of Books* 19.2 (2019). https://claremontreviewofbooks.com/giving-up-darwin/.

Gilmore, David. *Monsters: Evil Beings, Mythical Beasts, and All Manner of Imaginary Terrors*. Philadelphia: University of Pennsylvania Press, 2003.

Goertzel, Ben. "Will Artificial Intelligence Kill Us?" *London Real*, July 29, 2019.

Goethe, Johann Wolfgang. *Opinions on the World, Mankind, Literature, Science, and Art*. Translated by Otto Wenckstern. London: John W. Parker and Son, 1853.

Goff, Philip. *Consciousness and Fundamental Reality*. Oxford: Oxford University Press, 2017.

Goodrick-Clarke, Nicholas. *The Occult Roots of Nazism*. London: I. B. Tauris, 1992.

Grafius, Brandon. *Reading the Bible with Horror*. Lanham, MD: Lexington, 2019.

Grafius, Brandon, and John Morehead, eds. *Theology and Horror: Explorations of the Dark Religious Imagination*. Lanham, MD: Lexington, 2021.

Greene, Donald. "The Genealogy of the 'Man of Feeling' Reconsidered." *Modern Philology* 75 (1977) 159–83.

Greenstreet, Steven. "The Rendlesham Forest UFO Incident." *The Basement Office*, episode 5. New York: New York Post Productions, 2019.

Greer, John. *Monsters: An Investigator's Field Guide to Magical Beings*. Lewes, UK: Aeon, 2021.

Greve, Julius, and Florian Zappe, eds. *The American Weird: Concept and Medium*. London: Bloomsbury, 2021.

Griffith, Richard. *A Series of Genuine Letters between Henry and Frances*. London: W. Johnston, 1770.

Groeneveld, Leanne. "The Boxley Rood of Grace as Puppet." *Early Theatre* 10 (2007) 11–50.

Halperin, Victor, dir. *White Zombie*. Hollywood: United Artists, 1932.

Hamori, Esther. *God's Monsters: Vengeful Spirits, Deadly Angels, Hybrid Creatures, and Divine Hitmen of the Bible*. Minneapolis: Broadleaf, 2023.

Handley, Sasha. *Ghost Beliefs and Ghost Stories in Eighteenth-Century England*. London: Pickering & Chatto, 2007.

Harris, Sam. "Can We Build an AI without Losing Control Over It?" *TED*, September 29, 2016.

Hart, David Bentley. *You Are Gods: On Nature and Supernature*. South Bend, IN: University of Notre Dame Press, 2022.

Hawking, Stephen. *A Brief History of Time*. London: Bantam, 1988.

Heiser, Michael. *Reversing Hermon: Enoch, the Watchers, and the Forgotten Mission of Jesus Christ*. Bellingham, WA: Lexham, 2017.

———. *The Unseen Realm*. Bellingham, WA: Lexham, 2015.

Hendrix, Scott. *Martin Luther: A Very Short Introduction*. Oxford: Oxford University Press, 2010.

Hessel, Andrew, and Amy Webb. *The Genesis Machine: Our Quest to Rewrite Life in the Age of Synthetic Biology*. New York: Public Affairs, 2022.

Heyes, Michael, ed. *Holy Monsters, Sacred Grotesques: Monstrosity and Religion in Europe and the United States*. Lanham, MD: Lexington, 2018.

Hobbes, Thomas. *Leviathan*. London: Andrew Crooke, 1651.

Hodgman, John. "A Brief Digression on Matters of Lost Time." *TED*, October 21, 2008.

Hoffman, Donald. *The Case Against Reality*. New York: Norton, 2019.

Hunter, Jack, ed. *Deep Weird*. Milton Keynes, UK: August Night, 2022.

Hutchison, Sharla, and Rebecca Brown, eds. *Monsters and Monstrosity from the Fin de Siècle to the Millennium*. Jefferson, NC: McFarland, 2015.

Ironside, Rachael, and Robin Wooffitt. *Making Sense of the Paranormal: The Interactional Construction of Unexplained Experiences*. New York: Palgrave, 2022.

Irving, Washington. *Rip van Winkle*. New York: Dover, 2012.

Jackson, Frank. "What Mary Didn't Know." *Journal of Philosophy* 83 (1986) 291–95.

Jobling, J. A. *Fantastic Spiritualties: Monsters, Heroes and the Contemporary Religious Imagination*. London: Bloomsbury, 2010.

Johns, Cheryl Bridges. *Re-enchanting the Text: Discovering the Bible as Sacred, Dangerous, and Mysterious*. Grand Rapids: Baker, 2022.

Jones, Darryl. *Horror: A Very Short Introduction*. Oxford: Oxford University Press, 2021.

Jurgens, Dan. "Raising the Stakes." *Superman*, vol. 2, #70. Burbank, CA: DC Comics, 1992.

Kearney, Richard. *Strangers, Gods and Monsters*. London: Routledge, 2003.

Kengor, Paul. *The Devil and Karl Marx*. Gastonia, NC: TAN, 2020.

Kierkegaard, Søren. *Either/Or*. Vol. 1. Translated by Walter Lowrie. Princeton, NJ: Princeton University Press, 1949.

Kirk, Robert. "Zombies." *The Stanford Encyclopedia of Philosophy*. March 21, 2021. https://plato.stanford.edu/entries/zombies/.

Kowalski, Dean, ed. *The Philosophy of the X-Files*. Lexington: University of Kentucky Press, 2009.

Kripal, Jeffrey. *Mutants and Mystics: Science Fiction, Superhero Comics, and the Paranormal*. Chicago: University of Chicago Press, 2015.

Kubrick, Stanley, dir. *2001: A Space Odyssey*. Beverly Hills, CA: Metro-Goldwyn-Mayer, 1968.

———, dir. *The Shining*. Burbank, CA: Warner Brothers Entertainment, 1980.

Kurlander, Eric. *A Supernatural History of the Third Reich*. New Haven, CT: Yale University Press, 2017.

Lang, Fritz, dir. *Metropolis*. Babelsburg, Germany: UFA, 1927.

Lanier, Jaron. "There Is No A.I." *New Yorker*, April 20, 2023.

Laycock, Joseph, and Natasha Mikles, eds. *Of Gods and Monsters: Religion, Culture, and the Monstrous*. Lanham, MD: Lexington, 2021.

Lecouteux, Claude. *Witches, Werewolves, and Fairies: Shapeshifters and Astral Doubles in the Middle Ages*. New York: Simon and Schuster, 2003.

Levi, Steven. "P. T. Barnum and the Fiji Mermaid." *Western Folklore* 36 (1977) 149–58.

Levine, Janet. "Functionalism." *The Stanford Encyclopedia of Philosophy*. December 21, 2021. https://plato.stanford.edu/entries/functionalism/.

Lewis, C. S. Lewis. *The Great Divorce*. New York: HarperCollins, 2000.

———. "The Inner Ring." In *The Weight of Glory and Other Addresses*, 55–66. New York: Macmillan, 1949.

———. *The Lion, the Witch, and the Wardrobe*. New York: HarperCollins, 1994.

———. *The Magician's Nephew*. London: Macmillan, 1955.

———. *Mere Christianity*. New York: HarperOne, 2000.

———. *The Problem of Pain*. New York: HarperCollins, 1996.

———. "Religion and Rocketry." In *The World's Last Night and Other Essays*, 83–92. New York: Harcourt, Brace, & Company 1960.

———. *The Screwtape Letters*. New York: HarperOne, 2001.

———. *The Silver Chair*. New York: HarperOne, 1980.

———. *Surprised by Joy*. New York: Harcourt, Brace, & Company 1955.

———. *That Hideous Strength*. New York: Scribner, 1996.

———. "The Weight of Glory." In *The Weight of Glory and Other Addresses*, 1–15. New York: Macmillan, 1949.

Loeb, Jeph, and Geoff Johns. "The House of Dracula." *Superman*, vol. 2, #180. Burbank, CA: DC Comics, 2002.

Longinus, Cassius. *On the Sublime*. Translated by James Arieti and John Crossett. Lewiston, NY: Mellen, 1985.

Lovecraft, H. P. *Dagon and Other Macabre Tales*. New York: HarperCollins, 1987.

Lucas, George, dir. *Star Wars*. Los Angeles: 20th Century Fox, 1977.

Lynch, David, dir. *Twin Peaks*. Los Angeles: Propaganda Films, 1990–91.

———, dir. *Twin Peaks: The Return*. New York: Showtime, 2017.

Mack, John. *Abduction: Human Encounters with Aliens*. New York: Scribner, 1994.

Macumber, Heather. *Recovering the Monstrous in Revelation*. Lanham, MD: Lexington, 2021.

Mayor, Adrienne. *Gods and Robots: Myths, Machines, and Ancient Dreams of Technology*. Princeton: Princeton University Press, 2020.

McClelland, Bruce. *Slayers and Their Vampires: A Cultural History of Killing the Dead*. Ann Arbor: University of Michigan Press, 2006.

McGrath, James. *Theology and Science Fiction*. Eugene, OR: Cascade, 2016.

Mckee, Gabriel, and Roshan Abraham, eds. *Theology and the DC Universe*. Lanham, MD: Lexington, 2023.

McLuhan, Marshall. *Understanding Media*. New York: McGraw Hill, 1964.

McMahon-Coleman, Kimberley, and Roslyn Weaver. *Werewolves and Other Shapeshifters in Popular Culture: A Thematic Analysis of Recent Depictions*. Jefferson, NC: McFarland, 2012.

Melville, Herman. *Moby Dick*. New York: Dover, 2015.

Meyer, Stephen. *The Return of the God Hypothesis*. New York: HarperOne, 2021.

Milton, John. *Paradise Lost*. In *The Complete Poems and Major Prose*, edited by Merritt Hughes, 173–454. Indianapolis, IN: Hackett, 2003.

Missler, Chuck, and Mark Eastman. *Alien Encounters: The Secret behind the UFO Phenomenon*. Coeur d'Alene, ID: Koinonia House, 2003.

Mittman, Asa Simon, and Peter J. Dendle, eds. *The Ashgate Research Companion to Monsters and the Monstrous*. Burlington, VT: Ashgate, 2012.

Monod, Paul. *Solomon's Secret Arts: The Occult in the Age of Enlightenment*. New Haven, CT: Yale University Press, 2013.

Moore, Alan. *Watchmen*. Burbank, CA: DC Comics, 1986.

Nash, Ogden. "Dragons Are Too Seldom." In *Many Long Years Ago*, 14. New York: Dent, 1954.

Nietzsche, Friedrich. *Beyond Good and Evil*. Translated by Walter Kaufmann. New York: Knopf Doubleday, 2010.

———. *Ecce Homo: How to Become What You Are*. Translated by Duncan Large. Oxford: Oxford University Press, 2007.

NOAA. "What Is the Bloop?" National Ocean Service: National Oceanic and Atmospheric Administration website, October 5, 2017. https://oceanservice.noaa.gov/facts/bloop.html.

Oldridge, Darren. *The Devil: A Very Short Introduction*. Oxford: Oxford University Press, 2012.

Orwell, George. *1984*. London: Penguin, 1977.

———. "Some Notes on Salvador Dali." In *Collected Essays, 1943–1946*, edited by Ian Angus and Sonia Orwell, 156–64. Boston: Godine, 1968.

Paffenroth, Kim, and John W. Morehead, eds. *The Undead and Theology*. Eugene, OR: Pickwick, 2012.

Paley, William. *Natural Theology*. Edited by David Knight and Matthew Eddy. Oxford: Oxford University Press, 2006.

Pasulka, Diana. *American Cosmic: UFOs, Religion, Technology*. Oxford: Oxford University Press, 2019.

Paynter, Helen. *Telling Terror in Judges 19*. London: Routledge, 2020.

Peacock, Jess. *Such a Dark Thing: Theology of the Vampire Narrative in Popular Culture*. Eugene, OR: Wipf & Stock, 2015.

Petrov, Valentin Vasilyevich. "Did Yuri Gagarin Say He Didn't See God in Space?" *Pravmir*, April 12, 2013. https://www.pravmir.com/did-yuri-gagarin-say-he-didnt-see-god-in-space/.

Phillips, Kendall. *Kolchak: The Nightstalker*. Detroit: Wayne State University Press, 2022.

Pindar. "Seventh Olympic Ode." In *Pindar*, translated by C. A. Wheelwright, 36–43. London: A. J. Valpy, 1830.

Plato. *The Laws*. Translated by Benjamin Jowett. Oxford: Oxford University Press, 1892.

———. *Meno*. Translated by W. R. M. Lamb. In *Plato in Twelve Volumes*, vol. 3. London: Heinemann, 1967.

———. *Timaeus*. Translated by Donald Zeyl. Indianapolis: Hackett, 2000.

Poe, Edgar Allan. "The Tell-Tale Heart." In *The Dover Reader: Edgar Allen Poe*, 193–97. New York: Dover, 2014.

Polianski, Igor. "The Antireligious Museum." *Science, Religion and Communism in Cold War Europe*, edited by Paul Betts and Stephen Smith, 253–73. London: Palgrave, 2016.

Poole, Scott. *Monsters in America*. Waco, TX: Baylor University Press, 2014.

Pope, Nick. *The Encounter in Rendlesham Forest*. New York: Macmillan, 2014.

Ptolemy, Barry, dir. *Transcendent Man*. Culver City, CA: Ptolemaic Productions, 2009.

Puglionesi, Alicia. *Common Phantoms: An American History of Psychic Science*. Palo Alto, CA: Stanford University Press, 2020.

Purkiss, Diane. *Troublesome Things: A History of Fairies and Fairy Stories*. London: Penguin, 2000.

Reece, Gregory. *Creatures of the Night: In Search of Ghosts, Vampires, Werewolves and Demons*. London: Bloomsbury, 2012.

Rice, Jeff, creator. *Kolchak: The Night Stalker*. Universal City, CA: Universal Pictures, 1974.

Roberts, Hannah. "Spike Milligan's Gravestone Quip Is Nation's Favorite Epitaph." *Daily Mail*, May 17, 2012.

Ross, Gary, dir. *The Hunger Games*. Santa Monica, CA: Lionsgate, 2012.

Rowling, J. K. *Harry Potter and the Chamber of Secrets*. London: Bloomsbury, 1999.

Rubenstein, Mary-Jane. *Pantheologies: Gods, Worlds, Monsters*. New York: Columbia University Press, 2018.

Russell, Bertrand. "Why I Am Not a Christian." In *Why I Am Not a Christian and Other Essays*, 3–23. New York: Simon and Schuster, 1957.

Sartre, Jean-Paul. *No Exit*. In *No Exit and Three Other Plays*, translated by Stuart Gilbert, 1–46. New York: Vintage, 1989.

Schaefer, Karl, and Craig Engler, creators. *Z Nation*. Burbank, CA: The Asylum, 2014–18.

Schwebel, Lisa. *Apparitions, Healings, and Weeping Madonnas: Christianity and the Paranormal*. Mahwah, NJ: Paulist, 2014.

Sconduto, Leslie. *Metamorphoses of the Werewolf: A Literary Study from Antiquity through the Renaissance*. Jefferson, NC: McFarland, 2008.

Scott, Ridley, dir. *Blade Runner*. Burbank, CA: Warner Brothers Entertainment, 1982.

Shakespeare, William. *Hamlet*. Edited by Sylvan Barnet. New York: Signet Classic, 1998.

———. *Macbeth*. Edited by Sylvan Barnet. New York: Signet, 1998.

———. *A Midsummer Night's Dream*. Edited by Peter Holland. Oxford: Oxford University Press, 2008.

———. *Much Ado about Nothing*. Edited by Sylvan Barnet. New York: Signet, 1998.

———. *Richard II*. Edited by Kenneth Muir. New York: Signet, 1999.

Shatner, William, dir. *Star Trek 5: The Final Frontier*. New York: Paramount, 1989.

Shatzer, Jacob. *Transhumanism and the Image of God*. Downers Grove, IL: InterVarsity, 2019.

Sheldrake, Rupert. *Science Set Free*. New York: Random House, 2013.

Shelley, Mary. *Frankenstein; or, The Modern Prometheus*. New York: Random House, 2018.

Shyovitz, David. "Christians and Jews in the Twelfth-Century Werewolf Renaissance." *Journal of the History of Ideas* 75 (2014) 521–43.

South, James, ed. *Buffy the Vampire Slayer and Philosophy*. Chicago: Open Court, 2003.

Stark, Ryan. *Biblical Sterne: Rhetoric and Religion in the Shandyverse*. London: Bloomsbury, 2021.

Sterne, Laurence. *The Sermons of Laurence Sterne*. Edited by Melvyn New. Gainesville: University of Florida Press, 1996.

Stevenson, Gregory, ed. *Theology and the Marvel Universe*. Lanham, MD: Lexington, 2022.

Stoker, Bram. *Dracula*. Oxford: Oxford University Press, 2011.

Strieber, Whitley. *Communion*. New York: Beech Tree, 1987.

Stuart-Buttle, Tim. "Gibbon and Enlightenment History in Eighteenth-Century Britain." In *The Cambridge Companion to Edward Gibbon*, 110–27. Cambridge: Cambridge University Press, 2018.

Swift, Jonathan. *Tale of a Tub and Other Works*. Edited by Angus Ross and David Woolley. Oxford: Oxford University Press, 2008.

Thigpen, Paul. *Extraterrestrial Intelligence and the Catholic Faith: Are We Alone in the Universe with God and the Angels?* Gastonia, NC: TAN, 2022.

Thomas, Keith. *Religion and the Decline of Magic*. London: Weidenfeld and Nicholson 1971.

Thrasher, Andrew, and Austin Freeman, eds. *Theology, Fantasy, and the Imagination*. Lanham, MD: Lexington, 2023.

Toland, John. *Christianity Not Mysterious*. London: Printed for S. Buckley, 1696.

Tolkien, J. R. R. *The Monsters and the Critics*. London: HarperCollins, 1997.

Trimpi, Helen. "Melville's Use of Demonology and Witchcraft in *Moby Dick*." *Journal of the History of Ideas* 30 (1969) 543–62.

Twain, Mark. *Is Shakespeare Dead?* New York: Harper and Brothers, 1909.

———. *Mark Twain at Your Fingertips*. Edited by Caroline Thomas Harnsberger. New York: Dover, 2012.

———. *Twain's Speeches*. New York: Harper & Brothers, 1910.

Tyson, Paul. *Seven Brief Lessons on Magic*. Eugene, OR: Cascade, 2019.

Vallee, Jacques. *Confrontations: A Scientist's Search for Alien Contact*. New York: Random House, 1990.

———. *Passport to Magonia: On UFOs, Folklore, and Parallel Worlds*. Chicago: Regnery, 1970.

Virgil. *The Aeneid*. Translated by C. Day Lewis. Oxford: Oxford University Press, 1952.

Virk, Rizwan. *The Simulation Hypothesis: An MIT Computer Scientist Shows Why AI, Quantum Physics and Eastern Mystics All Agree We Are in a Video Game*. Palo Alto, CA: Bayview, 2018.

Walter, Brenda. *Our Old Monsters: Witches, Werewolves and Vampires from Medieval Theology to Horror Cinema*. Jefferson, NC: McFarland, 2015.

Weinstock, Jeffrey, ed. *The Ashgate Encyclopedia of Literary and Cinematic Monsters*. Burlington, VT: Ashgate, 2012.

———. *The Monster Theory Reader*. Minneapolis: University of Minnesota Press, 2020.

Whedon, Josh, dir. *Buffy the Vampire Slayer*. Burbank, CA: Warner Brothers Entertainment, 1997–2003.

Wheen, Francis. *Karl Marx: A Life*. New York: Norton, 2000.

Whitman, Walt. *Poems by Whitman*. Edited by William Rossetti. London: Chatto and Windus, 1901.

Wiley, C. R. "Lovecraft, Lewis, and Alien Worlds." *The Imaginative Conservative*, March 29, 2013.

Williams, Wes. *Monsters and Their Meanings in Early Modern Culture*. New York: Oxford University Press, 2011.

Winthrop, John. *The History of New England from 1630–649*. Boston: Little, Brown, 1853.

Wise, Robert, dir. *The Day the Earth Stood Still*. Los Angeles: 20th Century Fox, 1951.

Wittgenstein, Ludwig. *Philosophical Investigations*. Translated by G. E. M. Anscombe. Oxford: Blackwell, 1986.

Wodehouse, P. G. *Right Ho, Jeeves*. London: Barrie & Jenkins, 1978.

Wood, Gabby. *Living Dolls: The Magical History of the Quest for Mechanical Life*. New York: Faber and Faber, 2003.

Wood, Ralph. *Flannery O'Connor and the Christ-Haunted South*. Grand Rapids: Eerdmans, 2004.

Wyatt, John, and Stephen Williams, eds. *The Robot Will See You Now: Artificial Intelligence and the Christian Faith*. London: SPCK, 2021.

Yeats, William Butler. *Selected Poems*. Edited by Macha Rosenthal. London: Macmillan, 1962.

Index